~THE SECRETS OF Z

THE SECRETS OF ZELPHA

In which everyone has the deepest of secrets ready to be revealed.

Start Date: 10/07/22

End Date: 02/03/24

Written in memory of Emmy and Chester - my two beautiful cats.

~THE SECRETS OF ZELPHA~

ACKNOWLEDGEMENTS

I would like to thank my mum Jane Strafford for proofreading the entire manuscript. She has supported me throughout my journey of producing the book.

I would like to thank Drew Hanna Bannister for designing the book's front cover, spine and back.

Barbara Kielczewska, Karissa Joyce and Maximilian Kenko Yonderly have assisted with proofreading various pages between Chapter One and Chapter Five.

Phoenix Noble, Emily Caplette, Karissa Joyce, Kelly Marie Watt, Karen Souza, Cleona Allen, Jordan Knull, Elliot Smith, Lilly Jesso, Finn Chadwick, Amber Emily Cotterill, Alex Hardar, and Zora Lynn have also contributed towards the book.

Lisa Ellen Kelly and Marta Matos have supported me when uploading the book.

Special Mentions: *Darren S (dad), James W (friend), K Irving (Drama Teacher), R Patel (English Teacher), L Carey (English Teacher), H Kaur (Librarian).*

~THE SECRETS OF ZELPHA~

ABOUT THE AUTHOR

Molly Ellen Strafford was born in the United Kingdom, West Midlands. Throughout her childhood, she dreamed of being a YouTuber, as she loved watching gaming YouTubers online. She started with this and eventually moved over to Twitch as a streaming platform. Molly started The Secrets of Zelpha (her first novel) at 13 and finished when she was 15. Molly is now a Twitch streamer and an author, constantly creating for others to enjoy! With time, Molly hopes to sell copies of her books to the world and act out her own written scripts on stage. @xellengx @ellengaming

TikTok - @thesecretsofzelpha
Instagram - @thesecretsofzelpha
YouTube - @thesecretsofzelpha
Twitch - @thesecretsofzelpha
X (formerly Twitter) - @secretsofzelpha

~THE SECRETS OF ZELPHA~

CONTENTS

Chapter 1 **THE OUTCAST**

-Page 6

Chapter 2 **AWAKEN TO COLOURS**

-Page 23

Chapter 3 **SLEEPLESS ADVENTURES**

-Page 58

Chapter 4 **TIME TO PREPARE**

-Page 73

Chapter 5 **SHALL WE START?**

-Page 103

Chapter 6 **GAMES BEGIN**

-Page 122

Chapter 7 **CASTLE EXPLORATIONS**

-Page 136

~THE SECRETS OF ZELPHA~

Chapter 8 **THE DINNER**

-Page 146

Chapter 9 **HISTORICAL LESSONS**

-Page 153

Chapter 10 **CONFRONTATION**

-Page 161

Chapter 11 **DISCOVERY**

-Page 168

Chapter 12 **THE REVEAL**

-Page 188

Chapter 13 **RELEASE OF SECRETS**

-Page 195

Chapter 14 **FEAR AND CONFUSION**

-Page 202

Chapter 15 **THE FINAL GOODBYE**

-Page 222

~THE SECRETS OF ZELPHA~

~ 1 ~
THE OUTCAST

As her eyes slowly opened, morning sunlight streamed through the window. The white, sheer curtains drifted slowly above her head, only just tickling her nose and she could taste the sun's golden glaze on her lips. Sensing the sudden glare, she pulled the grey, woollen blanket over her head with an exhausted groan.

Must've fallen asleep on the sofa again, Ellen thought as she gripped it tighter. The scratchiness of the fabric suddenly reminded her that she needed to get a new, softer blanket. She'd owned this one for as long as she could remember - and it was quite worn.

She sat up, hair in disarray, and glanced out of the window. Raindrops still lingered on the outside, and she saw that her garden was coated in a delicate layer of dewdrops. The grass and crops were watered from the midnight showers, this made Ellen feel as though she could make the day a little

~THE SECRETS OF ZELPHA~

brighter. Today was an unusually beautiful day - the atmosphere around her being the most peaceful it had been in a while.

The clock quickly caught her eye; she sighed and pulled the blanket around her - it was too nice of a morning to waste lying around. She hauled herself up from the sofa and rubbed the sleep from her eyes. Arms stretched, she yawned as her thin, white nightgown drifted against her legs.

Her cat, Chester, was resting peacefully at the foot of the bookshelf. His ears pricked up at Ellen's footsteps, and he raised his head, curious to see if it was time for breakfast.

She made her way to the kitchen, keeping the blanket around her for warmth despite its roughness on her shoulders. Ellen stood at the worn kitchen counter before she felt soft black fur tickle her skin as he weaved between her legs. He purred as she rolled her eyes, aware that Chester was only giving her this much attention because he was hungry. She prepared Chester some raw fish and a bowl of water before shuffling over to the sink to fetch some water herself.

She was sure it would help refresh her mind from the stresses crashing down on her.

While the cold tap was running, Ellen searched for a large glass before catching sight of a framed photograph sitting on the windowsill. It was a family picture - *her* family. She examined the image that was taken so long ago. Tears welled in her eyes shortly before they fell onto her cheek. What she would do to have that family back again.

~THE SECRETS OF ZELPHA~

Ellen rubbed her thumb over the old photo as if she were comforting the people in the image. Tears were now streaming down her face, all her brain could focus on was forcing the tears from her eyes...

CRASH! She dropped the photo frame, startling Chester and causing him to race off towards the sofa.

The crash stopped the tears, stopped the sound, stopped everything. She quickly fumbled with the knobs on the tap and dried her eyes.

Mindset jolted, Ellen stared at the photograph sitting on her kitchen counter; the glass was cracked and the wood was splintered in the top left corner. She'd have to fix it later; running her errands today was the first thing on her list.

To her left lay files which she flicked through, although they were only making little sense to her half-asleep mind. Her mother's last will and testament - today's task had begun. So much had happened to her that she didn't know where to start. Ellen had recently discovered that it was a lot more difficult dealing with the mysteries of life than she'd realised.

Sighing, unable to take in any more information this early, she took the swept-up glass and chips of wood to her kitchen bin before preparing something to eat for herself. Maybe some harvesting would take her mind off of things.

Basket-in-hand and a piece of jam toast in the other, Ellen trudged through her garden with her brown coat and trusty boots, as well as Chester. She headed towards her berry

~THE SECRETS OF ZELPHA~

field to start her harvest. She had done this once a week since she was very young, always having some sort of company following behind her. Chester purred contently, happy that he could just keep Ellen company.

Ellen started picking as many berries as she could find. Blackberries, blueberries, raspberries, cranberries, strawberries—you name it. Only her strawberries and cherries persisted through the winter, most of the plants becoming dormant, but it was still rewarding to visit the berries and fruits. Something was refreshing she found from the experience of being out in the sunshine, surrounded by nature, and picking plump, juicy berries. Even though the berries she grew were delicious, she couldn't keep them all for herself; so she sold them. She regularly took a twenty-minute walk down to the local town to sell anything she grew or made; but not just fresh fruit. She found that she could do much more with them.

It wasn't long before she taught herself how to make homemade jams, wines, pickled fruits, face masks, and creams. Most of which she used on herself, the excess being sold, never wasted unless it was spoiled. They were a hit, but some townspeople in the nearby village started to keep an eye on her. They found it remarkable and strange that the products she made with honey and berries helped cure boils, bumps, and spots off the face. Ellen tried to explain that the fruits had special benefits (vitamins and such), but she was silenced by the argument that there was no way fruits could heal the skin.

~THE SECRETS OF ZELPHA~

Whispers and rumours of the words 'witch' and 'potion-maker' started to drift around the town, driving away potential customers, but Ellen didn't care. No matter where she went or what she did, Ellen was always an outsider; a stranger in her own skin. She tried to fit in, but it was never any use. Her differences were too great, and she was forever condemned to a life of isolation (other than her beloved Chester). Yet, she enjoyed this little life of quiet, cosy living. Although her customers dwindled every day, she was glad some people knew she existed for something not entirely negative.

The most Ellen had to deal with was nothing more than a few nosey children peeking over her fence and a couple of old men from the church in the town knocking on her door and trying to 'purify' her. She usually chased them off her property with an old rolling pin or broom. They had only bothered her a few times, but still enough to be a recurring annoyance.

After she had finished berry picking and harvesting her fruit trees, she headed back inside to make a few more jams. She stored the jars and containers in an old hand-weaved basket and started her journey to the town.

The dirt and gravel crunched beneath her feet as she walked - the cool breeze on her face and the sun peeking through the clouds were bliss. With a basket full of fruits and jams in each hand, she made sure to stick to the dirt road that led to the market in the village. It was a twenty-minute walk, and the first ten were through the woods. If there was anything in this world

~THE SECRETS OF ZELPHA~

she hated, it was being in the woods. As the trees gradually became more dense, she reminded herself to take a deep breath. She followed the thin winding dirt path and glued her eyes to the ground, occasionally looking up if she ever heard a sudden noise. All the bad memories - the endless nights of wandering through here with her mother came flooding back. It wasn't all bad, though. She still had good memories of this place; just the bad ones out-weighing the good. She remembered when she was younger - when she used to play in the woods with her mother. She used to roll around in the grass, collect all sorts of wildflowers, climb trees (try to, at least), and when lucky, find rabbits, deer, and foxes. For a moment, she wondered what life would be like if her mother were still here - if she were still alive. A feeling of melancholy washed over her. She couldn't change the past, and Ellen knew she couldn't.

Eventually, she made her way out; the sun blinding her slightly. She spotted the village ahead.

Ellen walked across the old bridge, and with each step, it squeaked and creaked. Crossing that bridge was like leaving the safety of her island refuge, venturing into the uncharted territory of a new kingdom where Ellen's mental map was blank, and the compass pointed to the possibilities that lay beyond the known shores.

One step into the village and there were people. Everywhere. *Busy for the morning, I suppose.* Ellen thought, hoping that she would have a chance to trade most of her goods.

~THE SECRETS OF ZELPHA~

She ventured across a very winding path to find a place to set up camp. To her left were two-story Tudor buildings towering over her. The area around her was crammed with stalls and barrels owned by those desperate to make some money. Then there were customers who either had very little money or were rich enough to shop in the buildings that submerged the market. After searching through the markets and keeping an eye out for a blanket, she spotted one. It was a soft, cosy-looking navy blue blanket. Ellen stared as she gradually walked past, thinking about how well it would look in her living room. She had barely enough for a stand that morning anyway. She approached a man with a long moustache and a thick accent she didn't recognise.

"Just one, please," Ellen asked, handing a small collection of coins to the man. He looked at the change in her hands and shrugged. Money was money, even though she was a few coins off.

"Here," he grumbled. "You can take this stand."
It wasn't much. It was made of dark wood, chipped in some places, and could easily give someone a load of splinters... but a stand was a stand, and she was thankful for it.

"Thank you very much, Sir." Ellen beamed as she started setting up her jam jars on display.

The man had never seen somebody so thankful for a rickety old stand like that. All of her items for sale were in their places, Ellen sat on the three-legged stool beside her. One person

~THE SECRETS OF ZELPHA~

after another strolled past her, and she decided to take action as some other merchants did. She had enough of being unnoticed.

"Ladies and Gentlemen!" Ellen announced to the crowd as the wind blew in her face. "I bet you have never seen products like these!" She continued to ramble on about how her products can 'cure the skin' and 'compliment a meal', using as much fancy jargon as possible. A slight success, she made a few more sales. However, within the crowd, she could still hear sneers and whispers, people hissing 'potion-maker' and 'witch', and mothers clutching their children even closer to them as they hustled past Ellen's stall. She couldn't let those words get to her; she couldn't let them tear her down. The only thing that eased her mind was thinking about her family, even though she knew she would never be able to see them again. She thought of her mother, and her brother James. It was how much she looked up to James, how much she wanted to be as confident and as strong as him that pushed her to keep going, day after day. She wanted to be just like him.

It had been a whole year since she had last seen him and she knew she had to follow in his footsteps and continue selling fruit just like he did, even though she believed they would never be reunited.

A few hours later, Ellen headed back home and grumbled to herself after having to walk back with not as many sales as she had hoped and the same old negative opinions.

Just another day with the same experiences and words.

~THE SECRETS OF ZELPHA~

This is so repetitive but hey - at least I sold some stuff, and that's what matters in the long run! Ellen thought to herself.

    She sat at the dinner table and thought for a few moments before deciding on something to eat. Ellen grabbed some eggs and struggled to turn her stove on before grabbing a pan to fry the eggs. She slid the eggs onto a plate and decided to grab some bread she had made a while ago - which had now turned a little dry. With a plate made, Ellen sat back down at the table and quietly ate her food, dropping a piece of egg to the floor for Chester.

    After eating, she stood up and dragged herself to do the dishes. Whilst washing the dishes, Ellen pondered about what she wanted to do next - suddenly remembering her blanket and the navy one she saw in the town. *That blanket is so old now, I should probably toss it out...* her mind began to wander while she finished the dishes, only being brought back to reality again by Chester rubbing against her leg and loudly meowing at her. She giggled at him as he weaved between her legs, trying to not hit him by accident as she moved away from the sink. Ellen grabbed his food bowl and filled it up.

    "I just gave you some egg-"
Chester had cut her off with his meowing as he strutted towards the food bowl that clinked against the tiles as it was placed on the ground. He ate with gusto as soon as it was within his reach, and Ellen huffed with laughter before picking up his now-empty bowl. She washed it and wiped down the kitchen counters before

~THE SECRETS OF ZELPHA~

heading upstairs to finish her day after storing her remaining products - hoping that tomorrow would be a better day, as always.

She headed upstairs to the storage room to put away what she hadn't sold that day. Ellen clutched the boxes tightly and slowly went up each step, careful not to trip on the stairs or drop anything. As she reached the top of the stairs, she walked down the wide hall, past two other rooms, and entered one with no door. It was filled to the brim with boxes and papers - and in the middle of the room was a small desk. She placed the top crate which was filled with empty jars on a shaky shelf, hoping that it wouldn't fall off. She dumped the rest of the boxes down onto the ground with a sigh and looked around. There were layers of dust; everywhere, the window looked filthy and was ready for a deep clean, and there was a build-up of spiderwebs all over. She pursed her lips together in exasperation. She'd clean out this room one day when she had the time.

Just before she reached the stairs to go back down, she noticed out of the corner of her eye, that the door of one room was slightly ajar. She froze. *That door should be closed...*

Slowly, she made her way toward the door and placed her hand on the doorknob. It was ice-cold. She couldn't move. Instead, she just stood there. Not closing it, not opening it any further. All she could do was stare at her hand clutching the doorknob. Her eyes were fixated on the shiny brass of the doorknob, as memories washed over her. She'd never come

~THE SECRETS OF ZELPHA~

upstairs to find the door of this room open. Not for the last year, anyway. *Why was it even open? Perhaps there was a gust of wind?* No windows were open upstairs. Whatever it was, it didn't change the fact that she had made a promise to herself. She swore she would never go into this room again. His room. However, here she was, wanting- no, needing to go inside.

    Snapping out of her trance, she inhaled sharply, closed her eyes tight, and gave the door a slight push. She heard it creek as it swung open, but she couldn't bring herself to open her eyes and look in. She couldn't. *I can't.* She thought, *I just can't.*

    From opening the door, a strong scent of rosewood filled the air. From the doorway, she saw the thick layer of dust on the furniture inside of the room. The overwhelming sense was the scent of the room. It was his. His room, his papers, his clothes.

    Her mind slowly drifted back to her memories of when she still had her mother and brother. Before the night of the storm, before he went missing. The happy days, where all they would do was play together; all day, every day. She looked up to her brother more than anyone, she dreamed of becoming as smart and courageous as him. He always wanted to be an explorer of some kind, he vowed he would travel the world and find as many new things as he could. She remembered how much they'd laugh together, their giggles echoing through her mind, and all the shenanigans they would get up to. Of course, they wouldn't just fool around; they'd help with the chores and prepping the products to sell, but Ellen remembered how much

~THE SECRETS OF ZELPHA~

they always looked forward to their visits to town. It was enough to put a small smile on Ellen's face, like re-watching an old videotape of her childhood.

Something suddenly clicked; she couldn't take it anymore. She needed to open her eyes. Slowly she did, reassured in knowing that nothing had been touched or moved. His papers; were still on his small desk, his bed made, his clothes still folded, his brown coat still hanging on the closet door, his compass-designed rug in the same spot at the foot of his bed - it was like he never left.

She closed her eyes momentarily, she thought back to the good days. Before the night he went missing. All her childhood memories about the two of them flickered through her mind like a movie. The giggles of the two of them, the soft and gentle voice of her mother. It all came crashing down on her in waves, Ellen grasped at her back pocket, reaching for the note. With blurry eyes, she ran her fingers along the creases of the worn paper that she kept on her ever since her mother had died.

'Open this when you're ready Ellen. - Mother.'

Was it time? She began questioning herself, ever since her mum had gone she always questioned if she was 'ready'. What did she even mean by 'ready'? How would she decide if she was 'ready'?

~THE SECRETS OF ZELPHA~

No. It was far too late for her to have another breakdown over this again. She should just sleep, that was normally what caused her to have these moments.

"Just go to bed Ellen," she mumbled to herself as she headed to her room - hesitating before shutting James's door. Smoothing down the note despite never actually opening it, she carefully put it back into her pocket and got ready for bed.

She once again felt the sun's golden glaze on her face the next morning, this time in the comfort of her bed, and sat up, preparing for the day. Just another day with a small number of sales - she was used to it by now in all honesty. Ellen sighed as she stretched and smacked her forehead to make her stop thinking negatively. Breathing in and out to calm herself, Ellen decided to finish getting ready.

"Okay Ellen, you know what... today might be different. Yeah! You're gonna sell tons of products and make them proud!" At the mention of the two she slightly deflated before shaking her head. *Enough of the negative thinking, they will be proud!*

She pondered off in thought as she brushed her soft multicoloured hair. Ellen went through the motions of getting dressed and such before walking downstairs to eat something and feed Chester his breakfast. She just made some eggs and toast which was most of what she had left in the house. Ellen realised that she was doing the same motions she did every day. *It is going to be like every other day, the same old motions and the same old*

~THE SECRETS OF ZELPHA~

people. Ellen sighed heavily as she finished eating and put her plate in the sink.

However, today was a day like no other. Suddenly, there was a knock at the door - a brief moment of silence. Ellen hesitated, not sure why she had visitors at this time in the morning - not even that - why she had visitors at all? Why should she even open the door anymore? The only reason people would come to her house these days was to ridicule and bully her. The thought of it made her immediately fired up. Another knock; louder this time, breaking the silence. She slowly crept towards it, Chester following like a bodyguard.

Ellen slowly creaked the door open, about a couple of inches, and looked down to see two young boys, no older than maybe ten or twelve. The shorter one (presumably the youngest) had fiery red hair and pin-prick freckles all over his face and arms. His green eyes looked up at her with innocence and curiosity. The other boy (*Probably the oldest,* thought Ellen) was taller and slimmer, with brown hair and pale skin. Ellen noticed the dark circles under his eyes and a healing scar on his cheek. She immediately recognised him, from when she was in town a couple of weeks ago. His family sold rugs and tapestries for a living in the town square. He had been hit across the face by his mother for failing to sell someone a rug. The ring on his mother's hand must have cut his face; Ellen had seen the whole thing unfold that day, much to her dismay. There was also a hint

~THE SECRETS OF ZELPHA~

of guilt on his face. He only stared down at his hands, never looking Ellen in the eyes.

"Um, excuse me," a voice pulled Ellen from her train of thought, and she became alert once more. She looked down at the youngest boy.

"Are you still selling your strawberry jams, Miss?" He asked eagerly. Ellen's brows furrowed with confusion. *Why were these children here unsupervised? Why had their caregivers let them come here willingly? Where were their caregivers? How could they be here without them?* Then a little spark of hope ignited within the very back of her mind. Giving her joy as she thought of it. Maybe, just maybe... they were being genuine.

She felt her lips curve up into a small smile, it was barely visible. But it was a smile; she hadn't remembered the last time she felt a real smile like that. Finally, someone who didn't think she was weird! That she was dangerous! However, as her smile grew, out of the corner of her eye she saw the brunette's face grow darker with guilt... and shame. He looked uncomfortable at his friend. What was wrong?

"MISS!" the youngest boy shouted, breathlessly. Refocusing on the centre of attention, Ellen responded with a sigh. Then looked him in the eye.

"Yes," she stated. "I still have plenty of strawberry jams I still need to sell. She mentally rolled her eyes, slightly annoyed with herself that she didn't get to sell as much as she wanted to yesterday.

~THE SECRETS OF ZELPHA~

"Can we come in?" The little boy chirped urgently.

"Well, I don't–" The two boys barged past Ellen before she could even speak, pushing her off-balance. The redhead rushed past with high energy, falling back onto the sofa and pushed her not-so-soft blanket onto the cold wooden floor. The brunette seemed more cautious about entering her house, stammering something unintelligible out. The redhead huffed and yanked the taller one onto the sofa, where he tried to sit politely. The shorter one slouched and sat comfortably. The redhead elbowed the brunette, who flinched. Rubbing his shoulder blade, he spoke quietly,

"We want to know where... that place is," He stated, with a little quiver in his voice. Sat with his back straight, trying to seem confident, but still scared. Ellen focused on his little hands which had now developed a small amount of shakiness.

THUD!

The shorter boy pushed his 'friend' off the sofa and to the floor. It wasn't a hard floor, as Ellen had a fluffy carpet, but still. He groaned in pain, and the impact of his fall knocked one of Ellen's jars off a shelf. Now with a boy, jam, and glass at her feet, she was red in anger. Why were they here? To destroy her house?! *I'm so fed up with this* she thought. The redhead took control of the conversation.

"We want to know where your witchcraft takes place!" Ellen, now quite disturbed by the boy's comment, headed over to

~THE SECRETS OF ZELPHA~

the ageing wooden drawer to grab her rolling pin, in preparation to chase them off her land. Another one, again.

"Why do you like being alone, just you and the small cat?" Chester purred at the sound of the word cat, still by Ellen's side, aware they were speaking of him.

"Where is your family?" There she stood, with one boy on the floor, another in her face - worried. Nobody mentioned anything that made her think of her brother, her mother, her old life, home. It had been so long, and so much had changed. It all came flooding back. A single tear dropped from her eyes.

"GET OUT!" Ellen began to chase them out. Fed up, that this was slowly becoming a more regular occurrence. However this time... this time, something was different. Refocusing on the real world, she realised both boys had shot up and ran out of the house - she began to chase them.

The two were running, out of the border of her property and into the woods surrounding her house. She chased them further into the forest, panting as she tried to keep the two in her sight. Suddenly, Ellen was stricken with a sickening feeling of nausea; her vision swirled - making the two boys disappear from her line of sight. The world was spinning around Ellen as she looked down. *What? How?* The floor beneath her feet started to disintegrate, she realised in fear and horror that the one thing keeping her stable was disappearing.

Falling.

~ 2 ~

AWAKEN TO COLOURS

THUD! Pain ricocheted throughout Ellen's body as she hit the ground. The force of the fall had winded her; she couldn't even cry out in pain, audibly at least. All she could do was lie there as she tried to steady her breath. After a couple of seconds, she slowly sat up and clutched her ribcage in agony. With uneven breathing and blurry vision, she looked up slowly to see where she had fallen from, only to find that she was looking up into an infinite void. Surely, Ellen should have died from that height. But why hadn't she? Instead, it had just left her with a bruised back, and fortunately no broken bones.

As soon as her eyes adjusted fully, her heart started racing as she sat up. Her eyes searched every corner of the small room she was trapped in - she saw nothing, it was all just darkness.

"W-what happened? Where am I?" She gasped, almost to herself. Suddenly, a blinding light burst into the room, spilling brightness everywhere and coating the walls around her. She

~THE SECRETS OF ZELPHA~

quickly shielded her eyes before opening them slowly. A large, metal gate was down in front of her, and she could hear voices - *people*.

Suddenly, an unfamiliar voice started to approach her; it sounded urgent.

"Excuse me, child! Yes, you!"

The heavy footsteps became louder as they got closer. Ellen could feel her heartbeat pulsing in her ear while her mouth became dry. She looked up to see an older woman, walking quickly toward her. She wore an off-white shirt that was tucked tightly into a long, floaty, dark-grey skirt that just reached her ankles, her silver-grey hair tied back into a slick bun, and a stern look plastered on her face. The woman looked stressed out - and quite scary, towering over Ellen, which caused a shiver to cascade down her spine. If Ellen was being truthful, she felt quite relieved that there was a barrier between them.

"Young lady, are you our contestant for the blue team this year?" Ellen wasn't listening, ignoring her. Instead, her eyes wandered to behind the woman, where rows of people who looked her age and slightly older; were sitting on wooden benches. All of their eyes were still on her, staring at her like she was from a different planet.

"Child, it's *rude* to ignore a question!" the woman scolded. "Are you or are you not our contestant for the blue team this year?"

~THE SECRETS OF ZELPHA~

Contestant? Team? Year? Is this some sort of competition? Where even am I? Have I been entered into a competition? Who entered me? She said year, does that mean I'm at a school?

Eyes. The dozens of eyes targeted Ellen as these questions continued to float around her mind. The only thing Ellen could do was stare, mouth gaped open slightly. Her wits suddenly kicked back in.

"Huh? Blue team? Contestant? Look, I-I'm not sure I understand—"

"—She must be Ms Gaunt. I'll let her out." a low voice interrupted.

Ms Gaunt... so that's her name. Is she a teacher?

A tall, male figure appeared behind Ms Gaunt; he seemed quite young, with messy dark red hair that covered his pale face, making it difficult to make out his features. He was very fair-skinned and dressed in all black.

There was a gate that was separating her and the sea of strangers, suddenly it dropped to the floor with a booming *CRASH,* causing Ellen to jump out of shock.

"Up off the floor, now. I'm sure you have working legs." Ms Gaunt instructed coldly.

Their eyes locked as Ellen scrambled to get up off the floor as quickly as she could. This woman, Ms Gaunt was one scary lady and certainly someone she didn't want to mess with.

~THE SECRETS OF ZELPHA~

"Name, please." Ms Gaunt demanded. It took Ellen a few seconds for her to reorganise her mind. She needed to ask questions... but she just had too many.

"Ellen ma'am. If you don't mind me asking, why am I here? Who are you? Shouldn't that fall have killed me? What do you mean by 'blue team'?" she said, rattling her thoughts and questions "I'm not in any team, and what do you mean by 'contestant'? I didn't sign up for anything!" Ellen interrogated the angry-looking lady.

"All of your questions will be answered soon. Don't worry kid." said the same pale-faced guy Ellen had heard before. He stepped out from around the corner and gave her a small smile, but it didn't last very long. He locked eyes with Ms Gaunt, the smile he once gave to Ellen had evaporated from his face, and went back to his blunt, cold expression.

"Ms Gaunt, we should continue with the assembly. I'm sure the other student will show up soon." He said in a hushed voice. He tried to take the attention away from Ellen so she could have the time to process the last few minutes.

"Yes, yes. Thank you, Gak. Come, Ellen! Quickly, now." Ms Gaunt ordered when she started to walk down the middle of the hall. As Ellen rushed forward to keep up with her, all eyes from the other pupils followed her with every step she took; Ellen then took another mental note.

Gak. His name's Gak.

~THE SECRETS OF ZELPHA~

"We've been waiting for you, Ellen. Took you long enough to arrive." Ms Gaunt said looking dissatisfied with the time, as Gak started to walk behind them still looking blunt behind his red hair. *Wait. What? How did these people know that I was going to arrive when I didn't even know it myself?*

"I'm sorry, 'waiting for me?'" Ellen asked cautiously.

Ms Gaunt began to question Ellen about the 'other member' of 'the blue team'. Believing that Ellen knew this boy.

"'Other member'?" Ellen thought again. *Why was she so adamant that I knew this mysterious boy?*

Ms Gaunt slowly began to express agitation the more Ellen began to repeat the simple questions aimed at her. Ms Gaunt continued to interrogate Ellen, with a stern frustrated tone. Intimidated by her, Ellen responded with a jumbled mess of Yes and No. The headmistress was now absolutely furious and distressed. *Why was she this way? I mean I know I've got a lot of questions but this woman needs to loosen up a bit. How am I supposed to know everything? I've just got here!*

"Oh for heaven's sake. Lord help me this year." Ms Gaunt muttered to herself as they both reached the front of the hall. Ellen could tell she already had enough of it all.

"Just sit down here, child," Ms Gaunt pointed to a wooden bench labelled 'blue team bench'.

Ellen obliged without any hesitation. She didn't want to annoy Ms Gaunt more than she already had from bombarding the woman with questions that seemed never-ending.

~THE SECRETS OF ZELPHA~

"If they're not here, then we must start without them..." grumbled Ms Gaunt as she made her way to the podium. Gak stood to the side of her.

"All of you should know your purpose here; if you don't I will be extremely disappointed. Please raise your hand if you are unaware." Ms Gaunt said, scanning the students as Ellen slowly raised her hand to be spotted by her.

"Of course, *you*. Where is your last teammate!? They're very late!" she asked, annoyed, and instantly shot a glare at the ceiling. To everyone's surprise, a young-looking boy entered the room flying using a pair of wings. The boy screamed out of happiness.

"YA-HOOOOO! YIPPIE!"

A voice cried from above. Ellen looked up to see a figure with a split dye of bright, purple-pink and brunette hair, with wings flying into the hall. Her mouth dropped open. *He was flying! How is that even possible?* He suddenly panicked and ran to the person closest to him, who just so happened to be Ms Gaunt.

"Excuse me, ma'am! This isn't the afterlife! Who are you? How did I get here? Why do your clothes look so funny?!" He questioned, screaming in her face.

"I beg your pardon? Firstly, remove that attitude. Secondly, the booklets are about to be given out, and you are extremely late!" She shouted and looked up at the ceiling once

~THE SECRETS OF ZELPHA~

again. The new student looked at his shoes, with a mumbled apology, slightly embarrassed.

"You may call me Ms Gaunt. Now, sit down; we will explain what's going on and introduce our staff team." She instructed him and he did as she said. He sat down next to Ellen, his cheeks slightly pink from his flighty entrance. Ms Gaunt ordered silence and the room obeyed. However, the one that didn't obey her order, was the new boy beside her.

"She sure is strict" he whispered, causing Ellen to stifle a laugh. Ellen liked the new boy and instantly realised they would gain a close bond.

Ellen gazed at him, it seemed that he wore a red oversized hoodie - which looked to be very soft -, black ripped jeans, and chunky white boots, which finished the outfit. She gasped as she noticed that he had heterochromia... and one was purple! PURPLE! Ellen was in awe at his eyes, never in her life had she seen someone else with an actual purple eye that wasn't a contact lens.

Eventually, both of the children turned their attention back to Ms Gaunt. As the woman continued rambling about booklets, the booklets she spoke of appeared in each student's hands.

Wh-WHAT! WAS THAT MAGIC? WHAT ON EARTH IS GOING ON?! Ellen thought in an insane amount of panic and fear.

Ms Gaunt gave a brief overview of the information held within the magical booklets and changed the topic to different teachers.

~THE SECRETS OF ZELPHA~

It made Ellen curious about the school-like aspect of this new and strange '*world*'.

"Now, for teachers, each staff member has been assigned to a different team from the previous year and will show you to your rooms today." The teacher stepped forward and got ready to announce each team's teacher. As she read the lists of names, lights floated around them. Suddenly a blue light boomed through the room… and all of the eyes looked at -

"Miss Yonda" the woman announced. She continued talking but the new boy couldn't stay quiet much longer, he leaned over to introduce himself to Ellen.

"I'm Nyx. Do you have a clue what's happening?"

Ellen shrugged her shoulders, almost apologetically as she was just as confused. All she knew was that Ms Gaunt was in charge. They continued their conversation, while Ms Gaunt continued her speech in the background.

She admired the skill of the boy sitting on her right, she asked

"How were you flying?"

Nyx continued to explain that he made his mechanical wings, using rocket boosts to propel himself forward. He took off his wings and showed them to her. Ellen held them, and once again looked in awe. Ms Gaunt called for Nyx's attention. Both Ellen and Nyx were startled, looking up at her, Ms Gaunt looked at the two with annoyance on her face. They both knew that they were caught not paying attention and now everyone's eyes were glancing at them.

"Are you talking during my speech?" Intimidated by Ms Gaunt, Nyx managed to scramble together with a quick apology.

"Uh no. Sorry, ma'am, I will be quiet," Nyx agreed, Ms Gaunt gave him a suspicious look but continued with her speech. He pushed a button on the wings which made them fold up as he slipped them into a pocket in a pack he was carrying. Ellen listened as best as she could despite her confusion and not understanding what honour Ms Gaunt seemed to think she had by being here. Eventually, Ms Gaunt stopped talking and the two students instantly turned to the booklet in confusion.

"Hey it says we have a third member," Nyx said, while he seemed to read the book rather than flipping through.

"Yeah? What's their name? Also who's the teacher, I have a lot of questions" Ellen asked while she looked over at his book.

"Some guy named James and Miss Yonda, but look, it has things like how long they've been here, preferred pronouns, hobbies, even preferred nicknames..." Nyx prattled on about more things in the book as Ellen's eyes widened at the name she wondered, for just a moment, if it could be *her* James. Ellen started to refocus herself on Nyx's talking "... but besides all that, I'm not entirely sure what the book is talking about."

Now fully refocused and she had forgotten about the coincidence, Ellen decided to help this boy out

~THE SECRETS OF ZELPHA~

"What about the teacher, what was their name?" As she said that Miss Yonda walked over to the blue team's bench.

"Hi there! I'm Miss Yonda. You're the new members of the blue team, right?" Ellen glanced at the middle-aged woman that was in her line of sight. Fair-skinned, she wore a soft white shirt, baby blue trousers, and straight brunette hair fell onto her shoulders. A sweet and sincere expression was on her face, and a soft smile rested on her lips. She could tell that this woman would make this place feel like home.

"Hey! You are our assessor, right? I'm Ellen." Ellen stretched her hand out for the teacher to shake, Miss Yonda smiled and shook Ellen's hand.

"It's nice to meet you, you can call me Miss Yonda for now though." Ellen nodded and allowed the teacher to continue.

"Ms Gaunt has a few more announcements to make soon. Until then, try to make some friends in the other teams, and if you ever need me, you will find me in the staff room. Also, before you go, there is one more member on your team. I just asked him to grab some books for me during the assembly."

Nyx and Ellen looked at each other in excitement. Ellen thanked Miss Yonda, and immediately turned her gaze towards the boy who entered carrying a pile of books, eagerly calling Miss Yonda's name.

"Miss Yonda! I have the books you asked me to get!" He announced and dropped them to the side, exhausted. Miss

~THE SECRETS OF ZELPHA~

Yonda's face was filled with guilt and relief. She responded with a happy,

"Thank you so much, James! I'm so sorry I had to ask you on such short notice, especially during the start-of-year assembly. I should probably take these now..." Her eyes widened seeing how many books there were.

"It's okay Miss, either way, it's the exact same assembly every year, and all the teachers are required to be there." Soon Miss Yonda picked up the books and made her way slowly toward the library.

Ellen suddenly ran towards the boy and looked at him from head to toe. She was stunned, she just stared up at him. Tears fell from her face. *Is it truly you? M-my brother?* She thought until... Ellen's mind went silent.

"James?" He engulfed her in a hug just as she started to bombard him with questions, she attempted to stop the tears but failed. She sobbed in his arms and began to gain the confidence to speak.

"What- what happened to you? I- I mean- What are you doing here? You're- you're alive? When we moved the branch you-" James interrupted her, he slightly crouched down and pulled her out of the hug; he placed both hands on the side of her arms. He then squeezed her tightly. *Was that good or bad? Is he warning me, or not wanting to let me go?* A huge smile was on his face.

~THE SECRETS OF ZELPHA~

"Don't worry about that now! It's just great to see my little sister." He then grabbed her into a hug yet again. Ellen was silent on the outside, but her mind screamed in pain. *He's oblivious, he's bloody oblivious! He knew nothing about me or... mum.* Her mother... her mind raced around. Until she realised, she was in the comfort of her own brother's arms. She had to protect him. Knowing that she instantly stopped crying and looked up at him, with a smile - both real and fake - spread across her face.

"I mean- Oh you're the other blue team member?" The girl attempted to change the topic, not ready to further inside what had happened in her world. To keep him safe and calm, for the near future. James was now happy that his sister felt more comfortable.

"Of course! Blue looks good on me you know" James smirked and laughed at his joke. A small smile appeared on Ellen's face, from seeing how happy he was. *Does he not remember?*

Nyx was sensing the tension from earlier and how Ellen still wasn't herself; with a combination of that and boredom - he cleared his throat to get the siblings' attention. Ellen turned and saw Nyx standing right beside her. She was slightly shocked to see him there - it was like Ellen and James were in a completely different dimension, let alone a world.

"Oh! I almost forgot. James, this is Nyx, the third member of our team. Nyx, this is James, my- my brother." Nyx's

~THE SECRETS OF ZELPHA~

mood changed yet again, sounding both joking and angry; after the meeting with James, she seemed to have lost all sense of emotion. Nyx started to yell.

"What?! You never told me you had a brother!" he gained some attention from others in the room, and Ellen sensed a glare that burned her skin. James - who was much calmer than Ellen - could tell he was joking around, so continued with jokey energy.

"Honestly! Yes, I'm Ellen's brother. I've been at Planet Zelpha for a year, so I can help- like a tour guide!"

Planet? This was a different PLANET?! This can't be real.
Ellen's brain felt tampered with; this kind of thing wasn't real. *Is this all just a vivid dream? Is it from going near James' room, it's a dream because I'm thinking of him again.* Ellen's thoughts were interrupted by Nyx asking James what happened at the school, taking the opportunity to learn some information. He responded by starting to explain a basic story of the school and how old it is. The two kids looked around with curiosity as this story wrapped around their brains.

"Vintage; I like it." Nyx giggled.
In the corner of Ellen's eye, she saw three children that were waving at James. Ellen felt both happy and scared that he had made friends in this new world, she once again gave him this half-real half-fake smile.

"Anyways, go hang out with some people and make some friends, I have my friends from the previous year here so I'm

~THE SECRETS OF ZELPHA~

gonna go say hi to them," James said whilst being dragged away by one of the friends, he gave Ellen and Nyx a quick wave and ran off. Ellen thought *Wait, James has been here for a whole year...* this place may look cool, but it's new, filled with a lot of people, and most definitely scary.

"Wait. What about going home? What about my cat? ARE WE GONNA BE HERE FOREVER!? NOOO! I DON'T WANT TO GROW OLD AND FRAIL WITH WHITE HAIR AND BE A HALF-DEAD, BREATHING, ROTTING CORPSE!!!—" Ellen blurted out without a thought until Nyx stopped her. He wanted her to calm down, he needed to reassure her that everything would be okay and that she wouldn't be here when she turned old and frail or a half-dead, breathing, rotting corpse...

"—OKAYYYY... let's just calm down. Why don't we walk around together and try to befriend some people?"

Ellen took a lot of deep breaths, a LOT of deep breaths, in an attempt to regain her stability after just having an absolute meltdown. After she had finally calmed down, she responded,

"Yeah, I guess... just anything to distract me from the thought of being here forever."

Well here came that distraction - a girl came walking towards her and Nyx, they'd never met her before or seen her.

"Oh hey there, you guys must be the new blue team members this year. Am I correct?" the unknown girl asked politely. Ellen hadn't seen this girl before, *I wonder what team*

~THE SECRETS OF ZELPHA~

she is on? She introduced herself, hoping to not make any enemies already.

"Yes that is us, I am Ellen."

He didn't want to be left out, Nyx excitedly introduced himself to the mysterious girl that somehow inferred well that they were new in the blue team.

"Oh, oh, and I'm Nyx!" He exclaimed with enthusiasm. He was excited to meet new people and make more friends, so excited that he couldn't just hold it all back.

The girl in front of Ellen had soft light brown wavy hair fashioned into high pigtails, the ends resting on her shoulder. A nice-looking white shirt went well with the yellow checkered pinafore dress. A sweet smile rested on her lips and a serene expression was on her face - she gave a warm and welcoming energy. Ellen glanced up and down and noticed most of her outfit screamed she was from a different team, she was confused - why was someone from a different team talking to them? Overall Ellen was confused.

"Well I'm Dusk, and I was wondering if you wanna be friends, I'm on the yellow team. Our team is quite nice, we can cheer you guys on at The Games." Dusk smiled. She had a welcoming smile, someone you could probably rely on but since Ellen wasn't too sure about everything right now she didn't dwell on it too much.

She didn't fully trust her surroundings; however felt it was best to be in people's good books, and started with Dusk.

~THE SECRETS OF ZELPHA~

She seemed sweet and she thought they could get along quite well.

"That would be wonderful, we could do the same!" Ellen replied to Dusk excitedly, happy she was able to make at least one friend outside of her team, and that it wasn't entirely aggressive and strict here.

"Yup!" Nyx added in. Yet again he didn't want to feel left out of everything, he had felt the need to say something so he could be part of the whole conversation.

Suddenly some girls in red clothes walk over. They were all dressed in red outfits, as though it had a meaning. They didn't seem as welcoming as Dusk did, Ellen felt a bit uneasy as they walked over. The girls seemed like those types of girls that were straight-up rude for no reason even if you haven't ever spoken to them before.

"Eck, well if it isn't new members of the blue team, and there with Dusk? How cute isn't it?" a girl addressed with a mean tone. *What was her problem? We were simply just standing here.* Ellen stuttered. I mean what else could she say? The girl seemed somebody you could never rely on for anything unless you looked and acted like her or just be one of her little minions. Well, either way- Ellen didn't like the energy this girl was giving.

"Oh well hi, I'm El-" Ellen started introducing herself. She was cut off by the sweet Dusk, who now sounded not as sweet as when they had first met. It's like her tone completely changed within a blink, what did she have against these girls?

~THE SECRETS OF ZELPHA~

"Ellen, don't make small talk with them, they are a waste of your time. So please just ignore them." Dusk stated with a stern and determined voice. It was certain that she was not happy. Ellen wondered why Dusk was so against this girl, had she done something to hurt Dusk or did they just not get along?

Dusk glared at the red team. Intimidated by the four of them, Ellen kindly asked if Dusk knew them since she was confused about why Dusk was so adamant that these two girls weren't someone you would want to talk to. However, she got spoken over by another one of the girls, who completely ignored Ellen's simple question. *I now see how Ms Gaunt feels.*

"'Waste of time?' That's a bit mean don't you think, Dusk? I thought we were all still friends." She smirked a sinister smirk. One that meant nothing but betrayal. Ellen thought it was a bit funny how suddenly this girl had a lot of confidence after standing behind the other girl the whole time.

Dusk looked disgusted at this comment. She was so angry it felt like steam started coming out of her ears and her face started going tomato red.

"Friends, you think we're friends? Definitely not after what you and Myrtle did." She scoffed.

Myrtle? That's an unusual name, what is it with this 'world'? Myrtle stood in front of her with a glare like no other. A haunting glare, it was aimed at Dusk. This was something only a person with pure anger could have. Besides this glare though, she was a pretty, young girl. She had a red crop top on, with ripped

~THE SECRETS OF ZELPHA~

black jeans, it looked as tight as anything. Myrtle's cropped top made Ellen realise, everyone but she and Nyx seemed to be in groups of three, and each group wearing the same colour... *Oh, I know! Myrtle must be in-*

"Red! Red is my favourite colour. Why couldn't I have been in red team" Nyx pouted like a little child.
-red team.

"Oh trust me Nyx, you wouldn't want to be on their team" Dusk gestured to them like they were objects, and then continued, "and you most certainly don't want to be friends with them." Myrtle seemed unoffended and kept her haunting glare, however, for some unknown reason she continued to argue.

"Ouch, that kinda harsh Dusk-y. What do you think Evelyn, should she be able to fight and talk to us like that?" Myrtle laughed. Dusk looked at her, extremely unamused. Ellen started to panic. Are *they going to get into a fight or something? What on Earth is going on?!* She slowly stepped closer and closer to Nyx who was also panicking at the situation right in front of their eyes.

"You gotta be kidding me, Myrtle. Evelyn would never in a hundred years join you and your goons let alone be friends with yo-" She froze as she saw Evelyn standing beside them, dead still. Myrtle burst into laughter but stopped instantly and insulted Dusk.

"Of course. I should have known that you of all people would have the smallest of brains."

~THE SECRETS OF ZELPHA~

However, Myrtle's sarcastic comments were not crucial to Dusk at the moment, - her friend Evelyn was. She looked like she couldn't speak - so she expressed herself through her eyes. She showed that she couldn't move, couldn't escape. She was stuck. Dusk tried to walk closer to Evelyn, the closer she got the more Evelyn attempted to shake her head, to warn her. The third red team member shoved Dusk to the ground.

"Scram, you- you little worm!"

Ellen and Nyx - who were very scared - helped Dusk up, instantly dragged her away from the situation, and got her out of the atmosphere, Myrtle's voice still boomed above all.

"WORM?! LARYSE?! Was that seriously all you could think of?"

Dusk looked down, Ellen wanted to create a conversation to help cheer her up but after all of the commotion, it was too overwhelming to have even said a word. Until Dusk suddenly shouts,

"They did something to Evelyn; I know it. I hope they all trip and fall flat on their face in front of the entire assembly!" Dusk paused with a sigh and continued with "Evelyn's one of the nicest people I know, she'd never join them willingly." *Join them? What does she mean by joining them?* She felt curious, so Ellen started to ask Dusk some questions.

"What did you mean by 'done something' to her? What could they have done? Cast a *spell* on her?" Ellen laughed at her comment about magic, with Nyx quietly joining in.

~THE SECRETS OF ZELPHA~

As Ellen and Nyx laughed, Dusk instantly made them stop their little giggles by telling them that everyone there has magic and can cast spells and she was serious. Ellen and Nyx tried their best to shake off this weird thought, although they looked pale and shocked at the idea. *Everyone has magic and can cast spells? How? Why can't I? Do I have to do something to get my magic?* As they thought of what was just said, Nyx mumbled to himself as he didn't know what else to say since the laughing stopped, the mood dipped and it became silent.

"Yeah... hilarious..." He said in a whispered voice. He thought hard about what else to reply with but his mind was blank. Nyx was clueless.

Tension started to build up rapidly, Dusk had sensed it quite fast - so she had thought to introduce Ellen and Nyx to her teammates to try and break the tension before it got even more awkward.

"Anyways, I have to introduce you guys to my teammates; they're pretty cool." She suggested in an attempt to stop the silence and get people laughing again or at least just bring the mood back up.

Ellen, who was deep in thought about the current situation, responded,

"Yeah..." until her mind snapped back into reality: "Oh, uh, sure! Sounds like fun." She spoke with more enthusiasm. *Why do they have powers and I don't? Does James have powers? What do I need to do to get powers like the others?*

~THE SECRETS OF ZELPHA~

Dusk responded and guided them to the place where her team stood. They all chatted with each other, not focused on their surroundings. Two yellow teammates were talking with James. Ellen instantly recognised the boy, he was the boy who had snatched James away earlier. As they walked closer, they could hear the conversation. It seemed quite interesting and the group sounded like they were excited about something, they already heard one of the yellow teammates get excited, saying,

"Dude! That actually happened?!" the other one jokingly and lightly punched the first one on the shoulder, whatever they were talking about it seemed like something crazy enough to get that sort of reaction.

"Why would he say it if it didn't? Stupid." The other teammate sarcastically pointed out. It was pretty obvious so the teammate rolled their eyes slightly and smiled.

Just then James spotted Ellen, Dusk, and Nyx approaching them and a small smile grew from the corner of his mouth. He was overjoyed to finally be able to be with his sister again, excited for the day they escape and go back home, to the time of Ellen, James, and their Mother.

"Yo Dusk what's up?" One of the yellow teammates asked while the other repeated the story of James going missing to Dusk.

"I see you've already met Ellen and Nyx! Ellen is my sister." James proudly states. He could never be embarrassed by his little sister like most siblings were, Ellen and James' bond was something quite different. He was more than glad to see her again, he missed her so much it felt unreal.

"Ahh, I see; that's how you guys know each other. That made sense now. Well, um- I thought it would be a good idea to introduce them to Coverly and Gale; we would all make a good group!" Dusk suggested without hesitation, and she nodded at the rest of the group. The two slowly wandered over to James and Dusk- while Ellen and Nyx stood behind her. Awkwardly, the four introduced themselves and complemented each other's features, like their hair. They couldn't think of anything else to say; it was awkward, and there were a few minutes of silence between sentences. Eventually, the group looked like they were having a lot of fun, but Dusk noticed the teachers looked like they were prepared to make more announcements.

"We'll see you guys around I guess, I think the teachers are making another announcement so you better go to your team's bench!" Dusk pointed out breaking the short silence.

A third mental note. Dusk, Coverly and Gale are the yellow team, and they're all very nice.

The teams waved goodbye to each other and walked back to their team benches. Just as the group sat down, Ms Gaunt entered the hall, with her strict look on her face, like always, and walked towards them.

"Hello, blue team members. I hope everything is going well. Have you two branched out and talked to any other students yet?" she asked coldly but also seemed a little curious.

~THE SECRETS OF ZELPHA~

Nyx, not quite used to the intimidating teacher's attitude, took a deep breath and thought about what to say. The first person to have the courage to speak to the intimidating woman was Ellen, informing the teacher about them talking to the yellow team and describing how they were quite nice and got along quite well. Then, Nyx was brave enough to ask the question that had been bothering him since he knew James had been there for a whole year.

"Ms Gaunt, since James said he's been here for a whole year now... we were wondering whether there's any way we could leave?" He questioned quietly

The hall went alarmingly quiet; he immediately got cut off by the furious old lady.

"—LEAVE?! YOU WANT TO LEAVE ALREADY?! I find that incredibly rude." She bellowed and yet again shot an angry look at the ceiling. Ellen tried to cover up this mess to let some ease off from Nyx since he seemed on the verge of tears. She didn't like seeing a friend upset like that so she sat closer to him and tried to reassure him without talking. Ellen quickly made up an excuse to take the attention away from him.

"Oh no, no Ms Gaunt! We meant nothing like that, all we meant was-" She reassured politely.

" -I know what you mean child" Ms Gaunt cut her off again and turned away, and she mumbled something to herself. *She gets angry so quickly. Really what is her problem?* After a few seconds, she turned back to the kids who looked like they'd just

~THE SECRETS OF ZELPHA~

seen a ghost. "When the teachers have finished their discussions, we will announce how the students get to leave," Once again she mumbled something like "If any of you even get to leave this year, that is." and turned around fully with an intimidating look.

Ms Gaunt walked away as she left the dumbfounded students behind. Before they could process what was happening, Mr Gallo stepped forward and began an announcement.

"Attention; everyone! As your second headteacher, it is lovely to see all of your wonderful faces here once again. It is also my pleasure to introduce the new students - Ellen and Nyx - to the blue team, and I hope they settle in well." Ellen felt her cheeks go slightly red from having the attention of all in the room once again.

"We have a few announcements to make before you all head off to your dorms. Dinner will be served at 6:30 pm sharp in the cafeteria; check the map in your booklets if you're unsure of its whereabouts; and please make sure you get there on time. Curfew is strictly 9:00 pm, and if anyone is found wandering about the school after hours they will be severely punished. The parts in the school marked in grey are strictly out-of-bounds areas for students without a pass, if any students are found in these areas they will also be severely punished. Tomorrow morning, Breakfast will be at 8:00 am sharp and I expect each and every one of you to be up and ready for tomorrow."

The silence in the room, once he finished, was deafening. You could have heard a pin drop.

~THE SECRETS OF ZELPHA~

"IS THAT ALL CLEAR?" Ms Gaunt asks, causing everyone to fix their posture in a flash and yell "Yes Miss!".

"GOOD! Mr Gallo! I need you to inform the new students about The Games and the trials!"

The headteacher continued to scream, and Mr Gallo had no other choice but to obey her. *Who wouldn't obey Ms Gaunt she's like a living nightmare.*

"We'll start The Practice Games at 9:00 am. After breakfast you will meet your team teachers in this hall; they'll lead your team out to where the first practice challenge will be held. We'll start the real challenges when each of you has proven you are ready. The Practice Games are just there to train you for the real ones which play out a bit differently. For every challenge, a coloured team will be eliminated until the final two face each other off and proclaim the winner of the year. These Games include testing your speed, strength, agility, reflexes, and of course, your magic... and with that I am ecstatic to announce that the preparation for The Games of 2024 has officially begun!"

The room immediately started to fill with the children's hushed voices, including Ellen's and James'. They spoke about the 'magic' side of The Games, it made Ellen anxious. *What happens if they find out I don't have magic? Will I have to stay until I get magic? Oh my gosh, I'm going to die here!* Ellen's breath quickened.

~THE SECRETS OF ZELPHA~

"James, how are we supposed to win these challenges?" Ellen asked with a shaky voice.

Panic flooded Ellen's mind, *this magic stuff isn't real, what are people talking about?* James' facial expression turned angry instantly, his eyebrows pointed downwards.

"Keep your voice down," James demanded quietly. "Do. As. I. Say." He continued to demand in a strict tone.

Ellen was taken aback by the sternness in James' tone. He had always been sweet with her, Ellen was his little sister but even if he was annoyed, he never behaved in this manner. *What's gotten into him?* James had always been the caring older brother type, he's never tried to parent her or made her behave in any way he wanted, and he's not ever tried to control her or anything. *Why is he acting like this now? Maybe he's just trying to care for me? What if he's changed, what if he's not the older brother he once was? This world has changed him.* Ellen's mind raced; it wasn't understood why James suddenly spoke to her in that way. All the questions were louder than Ms Gaunts; "Alright everyone settle down" but they then were shattered into a million pieces by Ms Gaunt.

"I SAID SETTLE DOWN!" The entire hall went deadly silent, not a peep came out of any student, and Ellen's questions went quiet too. Mr Gallo ended his announcement, he explained that if you won The Games you were able to return to your home worlds, however, if you lose you must compete again next year. All students began to applaud as Mr Gallo stood back on

~THE SECRETS OF ZELPHA~

his green platform. The applause startled Ellen since she was still in her little world but she joined in as quickly as possible, hoping that she didn't get spotted by Ms Gaunt so she would have a little less disdain for her. Ms Gaunt stepped forward and explained,

"Your assigned teacher will now take you to the student dorms. But remember what we said about curfew! SEVERE PUNISHMENTS!! Gak is on watch tonight... GAK!"

Ms Gaunt was exhausting enough for Ellen alone, but poor Gak responded with the most tired "I heard you" possible. Ms Gaunt demanded,

"Oh. Right. Now that everything's settled... TEACHERS, ESCORT YOUR STUDENTS TO THEIR ROOMS! AND NO DILLY-DALLYING! GAK, PUT THE KETTLE ON! I NEED SOME TEA, I HAVE A HEADACHE! DISMISSED!" Ms Gaunt bellowed at the top of her lungs.

Chaos. Everyone was moving, everyone talked to one another, whilst Ellen felt like she was stood statue-like in the middle of a crowd. It reminded her of home, except this time she was not alone. She turned to her right to see that Nyx was also stood statue-like. She was no longer an outcast, she had what someone may call a friend. Smiling - she grabbed Nyx's hand and pulled him out of the crowd - using her other hand to reach around for James through the sea of people.

She grabbed James's hand tightly, with Nyx following behind. He pushed through the crowd to reach Miss Yonda -

~THE SECRETS OF ZELPHA~

who was calling for them to hurry up and follow her. Once they had reached her, they started to chat about how they were nervous about The Games and confused but also excited.

"That's the spirit, there's nothing to worry about! If you try hard, you're sure to do well. Practice made perfect! Let's get you to your room." Miss Yonda ended the conversation with a sweet smile and look that made you believe you could do anything in this world, while she tried to lead them out of the flood of people. Finally, out of the crowd, James decided to start up the conversation again.

"Miss? The library hours are still the same as last year, right?" He asked politely.

As the conversation continued Miss Yonda gave James a one-time library pass. Ellen and Nyx started to look into other team rooms. Nyx spotted the green team's room; the carpet floor was a green hue - imitating grass while a fake campfire lit up the room. A mass of vines and leaves hung from the ceiling - pink flowers sporadically placed, decorated the beautiful mess. Three dark oak beds were lined up near each other, with soft green blankets on top.

"What do you think our room will be like?" Ellen asked; while she looked into the room opposite with curiosity, she thought the rooms were magnificent and different in so many ways that each room was just as unique as the other. Nyx's mind started whizzing, he thought about all the different things blue, he hadn't seen that much of one colour in a room in his entire

~THE SECRETS OF ZELPHA~

life. It was all so new and also something he would have to get used to, quickly too.

Nyx started to mutter as his imagination went rampant - painting pictures within his mind. He imagined the walls would be soft deep turquoise, the ceiling decorated like the night sky - stars dotted the deep bluish-black drop and the stars even emitted little lights like night lights. The floor would be beautiful crystal blue flooring, complimenting the whole room and bringing it together. Nyx hopped up and down, he held in his excitement as he strongly gripped Ellen's hand, it made her wince with the pressure. He was so excited to see the room he would share with his new friends! One thing's for sure, this boy couldn't wait!

"Well, you don't have to wait much longer, because we are here" Miss Yonda looked behind her to check on the children, and her soft smile slightly grew from seeing their excitement. James who was just as excited as the others shouted,

"Open the door, Ellen! Quickly! I get first dibs if there's a bunk bed!" He then pushed Ellen into the door and it quickly creaked open. As she examined the four walls surrounding her - they looked barely stable - her smile dropped to the cold floor.

This so-called 'room' was pretty much a cave with three sad-looking beds, with one small dingy lantern sitting on the floor. The air was cold, in temperature and emotion. Dull grey walls surrounded them, it sucked all the colour away from their imagination. Sharp stalactites hung from the ceiling; James

~THE SECRETS OF ZELPHA~

wrapped an arm around Ellen's shoulders - dragging her closer to him for protection. A musty smell permeated the room, they glanced around the room to find the source. *Drip, Drip, Drip.* In a small corner was a puddle formed from water falling from a crack that was in the ceiling. Ellen gasped as her excitement turned into disappointment and dread, besides her, she heard James mutter under his breath - he thought that only he heard himself, but Ellen could just barely hear him.

"I can't believe I made this happen..." He was shocked, he forgot about what had happened to the room. He was so excited about seeing Ellen again after a year he completely forgot about the mistake he'd made.

Miss Yonda explained to them that if she could let them stay somewhere else she would but the students must sleep in their assigned dorms. Ellen froze; she didn't know what to think or do. However, she kindly added to the collection of lanterns on the side, to help light up the room around them before she rushed out of the messy room. Suddenly, a loud BONG shook the room and Nyx; held onto James for his life. *What was that?* Five more sounds followed after, meaning it was 6 pm. *Not long until dinner. Yay!*

"We have thirty minutes until dinner." Ellen reminded the group, as they all flopped onto their beds. A knock at the door startled James, which caused him to fall off his bed. Being the only one not sat and closest to the door, James sighed, stood

~THE SECRETS OF ZELPHA~

up, and walked towards it. He opened the door to see Dusk outside of it.

"Hey! What's... up...?"

Dusk slowly finished her question whilst she examined this cave-like room with a ceiling that dripped continuously. She slowly brought herself back to the conversation.

"Well, anyways; dinner's in fifteen minutes. Wanna walk upstairs together? We don't wanna be late!" Ellen saw Coverly and Gale standing beside her, they both waved at the blue team with a smile on their faces. The two teams met up and walked through the corridor and up the stairs together to the cafeteria hall. Nyx decided to start the conversation with the food.

"Whatever they're cooking, I can smell it from here; and it smells good!"

The six of them continued to talk about how there wasn't any cooking done, and the food was made by magic. James then began to joke around as he spoke about his exquisite taste.

"Yeah, the food's actually pretty good here!"

Ellen responded with a snort and then asked him,

"Did they need to get your approval or something?"

She missed this, they got along so well and after a year of not being able to talk to him, it was so lovely to be able to joke around with her brother, and not be upset by something as simple as the thought of him.

~THE SECRETS OF ZELPHA~

"Of course they do; I have exquisite taste!" He responded sounding snooty and confident. The both of them tried not to laugh at his comment.
Whilst they joked around Gale burst out with,
"I bet I have better taste than James" Without missing a beat, the siblings burst out laughing. They still held confident energy, James responded,
"I don't think that's a bet you're ready to make" with a small laugh. Coverly saw this as a perfect opportunity to join in the conversation, which made Ellen feel more comfortable with the group, as they were all able to join in with a joking scenario.
"Guys, guys, let's not fight, shall we? I'm sure you both have exceptional taste... but I think we can all meet on even ground and agree that mine's better than both of yours" she stated with a hint of sarcasm.
Nyx shifted his body to face Coverly, he looked her in the eyes and smiled.
"I like you! Why haven't we been friends sooner?" Coverly dramatically lifted her hand in the air and bent her knees.
"Fate kept us apart!"
The two snorted at the little performances. Ellen rolled her eyes, giggling.
"I think Nyx likes Cove more than me now," She said following on with a little laugh. Nyx gasped before he replied,

~THE SECRETS OF ZELPHA~

"Awww, don't get jealous Ellen! Cove's just cooler than you... that's all!" He faced Ellen with a small smile to see her have a deadpan expression. She wasn't finding this situation funny.

"Gee thanks, Nyx," Ellen said with a sarcastic smile. The two teams entered the cafeteria and continued small talk. All but Ellen. She was admiring the four walls around her, she had never seen such a magnificent room. *How could an overgrown 'mess' be so beautiful, and fit in the walls so perfectly?* Soft brown wood with greenery and floral arrangements surrounded many different tables. Each table was of a darker wood than the walls encasing them with dimly lit candles settled on them to give ambience. Green moss-like carpet trailed from the entrance and toward the back of the room - ending right before the magnificent brick fireplace. Near said fireplace, more floral peaked through the wood - giving more life toward the back.

"Now, where should we all sit? We have to sit together; no questions asked" Nyx stated. As he scanned the cafeteria with his eyes for empty tables.

"No way really? It's not like we're in the same friend group or anything" Dusk said sarcastically and rolled her eyes. Unimpressed by the sarcasm Gale said,

"Here's a good spot"
He saw that Ellen wasn't quite involved in the conversation and felt the need to make sure she didn't feel left out, or unwanted,

"What do you think Ellen?" He asked while turning to face her.

Ellen refocused on the group and replied with

"Yeah this is good, there's plenty of space here" As she agreed, the whole group sat at the selected table.

Before long, more students flooded the cafeteria hall, leaving the two teams feeling thankful that they were early, and managed to get a good spot quickly.

"How are we supposed to get our food? Is there a line we need to get into or something?" Nyx wondered, looking around. Gale and James on the other hand looked at each other with a smirk spread across their faces.

"Three... Two... One.." They counted backwards together. On 'one', bowls of creamy mushroom stew appeared, with six glass cups, a jug of ice-cold water, and a loaf of freshly baked bread. Nyx and Ellen's eyes widened at the sudden appearance of items on the tables. James smirked at their reaction, and Gale rubbed his hands together with a big grin before he looked at the two with their mouths opened in shock.

"Let's eat?" He questioned the two. Before he finished his sentence, Nyx immediately grabbed a bowl of stew.

After completely stuffing his face with food, Nyx suggested that the three head to their room early. Since they felt sleepy, the siblings willingly agreed and the teams parted ways for the night. As soon as Nyx reached the dorm he flopped onto his bed as though it was the heaven he had been searching for this whole time.

~THE SECRETS OF ZELPHA~

Ellen turned over to see her brother snuggled in his blanket, in an attempt to get cosy in this stone room. It had been so long since they had slept in the same room, if there was ever a storm she would get in with James rather than her mother. Her mother had enough to deal with and James was more than willing to spend the night with her. *What would life be like if I had done that the night of the storm?* Ellen reached into her pocket and grabbed the letter which was hidden away. It was all she had left of her mother, and now also her homeworld. *'Open this when you're ready Ellen. - Mother.'*

Was it time? Ellen went to open it until Nyx began to talk.

"Oh, I ain't sleeping - not after this much coolness." James giggled to himself.

"Oh boy." He faced away from Nyx's bed. Nyx grinned at James and Ellen, he put his arms behind his head as he lay down.

"I'm gonna stay up all night, mentally preparing for The Games and all, but I am telling you; I'm not... going... to..." His eyes slowly closed, cutting off the rest of his sentence as the rush of the day's events and what had all happened within a few hours faded away as he drifted peacefully to sleep.

~THE SECRETS OF ZELPHA~

~3~

SLEEPLESS ADVENTURES

Nyx's snoring boomed throughout the school, although the other students could sleep - Ellen began mumbling to herself.

"No... no. Please... don't... NO!" Ellen shot up instantly, then looked to her left she saw Nyx still snoring obliviously, she looked at the bed ahead of her to see it was empty, she couldn't find her brother anywhere in the dorm.

"Where's James?" She frantically asked aloud in the hope of a reply, however, Nyx only responded with a snore, followed by another snore.

As Nyx was no help whatsoever, Ellen began to leave the damaged stone dorm; it was vital for her to find her brother - to look after him - and she couldn't lose him again.

This panicked her, she always needed her brother, as she had learnt... she couldn't live without him any longer. She wandered around - for what felt like forever, calling his name until she suddenly got a whisper of a response.

~THE SECRETS OF ZELPHA~

"Sorry, excuse me professor—Ellen?" Ellen was shaken, she stood still for a moment. She thought she had been caught, Ellen was looking at her feet the whole time, and she eventually plucked up the courage to look up and see whoever was standing before her. To see this was no teacher but instead-

"Myrtle? Why are you here?"

Regret. She instantly regretted her decision to say a single word. Myrtle's eyes glared down at "innocent" Ellen before she bluntly stated.

"I could ask you the same thing."

Myrtle had instantly sent a shiver down Ellen's spine, her main objective was to avoid a confrontation with a teacher never mind Myrtle. Myrtle was worse than a teacher!

"Oh, right. Have you seen James? I'm looking for him." She anxiously questioned.

Myrtle looked slightly fumbled at the name, as though she was trying to avoid speaking about him.

"Who? Sorry, I can't say I have," she responded.

Ellen could tell Myrtle was dodging the question but she was far too intimidated by Myrtle to comment on it.

"He isn't up there, is he? What are you doing here anyways?". Myrtle shot a look at Ellen causing her to realise she had taken one step too far. This wasn't any of Ellen's business to know, all she wanted was to find her brother and leave. That's when Myrtle caused Ellen to realise that she was in the exact same situation as her - wondering about outside of hours.

~THE SECRETS OF ZELPHA~

"I'd rather make sure my brother is okay instead of worrying about getting caught." She decided continuing her search for James was the right idea, but Myrtle was one large obstacle in her way.

"Just use your magic to track where he is." A silence shattered all sense of atmosphere in the room... until- "James, was it?".

The silence made Ellen realise Myrtle thought she didn't have magic, and she was right. *What should I say? She's right... I don't have magic.* Anxiety flooded Ellen's mind, and her breath quickened. She had never been in such a predicament before, she could drop to the floor in tears and tell Myrtle all of her secrets and reveal her lies. It was not time. Ellen had to get to her brother - her safety - but was physically, mentally and emotionally blocked by Myrtle.

"I'm curious to see how strong yours is... you don't seem like the type of person to have strong magic like me." She sniggered mischievously. Again, the silence echoed through the atmosphere that had finally reentered the room.

"Let's see it then. Use your magic to track where this kid is." Myrtle impatiently blurted out. Once again, anxiety flooded Ellen's mind, it went blank until the long day and late night caught up to her.

"Oh! It doesn't work well at night, or when I'm sleepy! I can't cast a spell right now! I-I think I should go back to my dorm; I'm sure he'll be back there by tomorrow morning anyway." Ellen stuttered and looked around hoping to find an escape from the situation. She already felt stressed and the fact that she didn't know where she was, added to the pile.

"Uhm... do you know which way the dorms are?" Myrtle uncontrollably blurted out a laugh, then butted in her laughter with,

"You're lost?" Ellen tried her best not to blush a bright red, somehow making her flesh a light pink shade all over, she managed to have said some form of 'yes' whilst stumbling over her words. A smile spread across Myrtle's face, it looked like some form of a sarcastic smile, a smile that looked like it had a bad idea behind it. However, Ellen went along with her plan.

"I don't think pointing will do you any good, but I can show you the way... so I'll walk with you." Myrtle offered, leading with her smile.

"Thanks, I really appreciate that!" Ellen naively responded. Myrtle started to walk up the stairs beside her, and Ellen followed. Realising that she had not seen where she was going before and it didn't look like the way she was taken by Miss Yonda. She asked unsure if she should still follow, but all Myrtle could respond with was the topic of magic. The topic of this 'fantasy' people tried to drill into Ellen's mind.

"We don't allow non-magical people into this place, if a non-magical person is found here we have to hand them into Ms Gaunt." Before arriving at their destination, Ellen learned that non-magical beings - such as herself - would be sent to the jails.

~THE SECRETS OF ZELPHA~

Simply for not having magic. After a lot of walking - that left Ellen with sore legs - they arrived at a heavy-looking iron door.

"Here we are; if you walk through this door it will bring you to whatever room in the school you think of." Ellen peered through the small gaps in the door, each surface was black. Around the room were buttons and levers and magical dust organised in a pattern Ellen could never begin to comprehend, it was this magical dust which caused the room to have a slight illumination.

All Ellen thought was about the jails, so she walked into the room without even thinking. The door snapped shut as soon as her body crossed the threshold.

"And just to add to your little 'adventure', that room is considered a grey area. Have fun facing severe punishments, Ellen!" Myrtle ran off, out of Ellen's sight in seconds. Ellen's instant reaction was to cry for help.

"Is anyone there? Please! Please, help me!" While she called for help, Gak rushed up the stairs, alerted by the noise, and saw her in the room. Gak's eyes landed on Ellen. *Oh no* she thought.

"What do you think you're doing in an out-of-bounds area?" he said in a stern aggressive voice. Stumbling over her words Ellen managed to create a quick jumbled-up mess.

"-I'm so sorry Sir. You see, a member of my team went missing, then a girl in red team sort of—" she stopped, his eyes

~THE SECRETS OF ZELPHA~

glared at her, not quite the same glare as Myrtle's, but a glare nonetheless.

"—That's enough. I don't want to hear anymore." he paused, considering his options here

"Ugh—let me get you out of there..."
A wave of relief hit Ellen in the face, however - she was still somewhat unsure, this man was being nice but his facial expressions and looks gave off a different impression.
After he fiddled with a handful of crystals, he held one near the door and it automatically opened with a loud creak. Gak told Ellen that he must send her to the student dorms but first must go to the teacher's lounge. All of a sudden, Ellen began to stare at Gak... intensely. The stare caused him to take a step back in confusion.

"How old are you? You look only a few years older than me..." This comment caused Gak's pale face to finally have a bit of colour to it. He stumbles over his words, talking about the lighting, and how Ms Gaunt wanted younger teachers for the students, leaving Ellen feeling quite suspicious. Eventually, his face went back to his blank look as he made himself a drink.

"Fizzle Juice?" He shoves said 'drink' in Ellen's face. It was bubbling a luminous purple colour, with a layer of froth at the top. Not wanting to be poisoned, Ellen politely declined the offer, while Gak started to create small talk as he continued to enjoy his drink.

~THE SECRETS OF ZELPHA~

"Now, you mentioned someone had wandered off. Who exactly are you looking for?" he questioned. Still horrified by the strange concoction 'fizzle juice', Ellen responded.

"James, he's one of my teammates." Suddenly, some form of faze washed over Gak. The shift in his tone was not very sudden, but also not smooth - as it changed to a monotone grey tone, it turned dull and even dead. Gak's facial expression matched his voice, his eyes widening a little before calming back down. Gak told Ellen what she desperately needed to hear.

"He's in the library," he said in a quiet monotone voice. This immensely unusual yet vague comment and expression made Ellen completely forget about the terrible froth bubbling to her side.

"Huh? What made you say that? He could be anywhere..." Suddenly Gak went back to himself as if something snapped back into place. He questioned what had happened, the way he spoke it was like he had no memory of what just happened.

"You just said he's in the library, James?" A smile appears on Gak's face.

"Oh! James. He will definitely be in the library, great idea Ellen! You know what James is like." he nodded. Ellen continued to ask Gak where the library was causing him to put his drink on the table beside him, making a disappointed sigh in the process. making Ellen give it one more sceptical look.

~THE SECRETS OF ZELPHA~

"I would recommend trying to learn how to navigate on your own before you go on any more midnight adventures," he said, a tinge of frustration in his voice. Ellen said she would and followed him to the library. Curious about why he's been acting so strange, Ellen decided to ask Gak a bit about himself

"So... how many years have you taught at this school? Did you attend this place too? Did you go here and then become a teacher here or—" He gave a stern expression causing Ellen to stop.

"No, it's alright. I''s only natural for your kind of people to ask questions." *He's found out, he has finally discovered I have no magic... What should I say? Just say something, Ellen!*

"M-my kind?" She looked at Gak, and her skin tone started to go as pale as his.

"You're in the blue team, are you not?" He continued to talk about how he picked up on the fact that blue team members always asked the most questions about the place and that he picked up on it a few years ago. Ellen mumbled something under her breath and then looked Gak in the eye and said,

"Professor Gak, could you just... answer... one of my questions?" He looked at her, with a face that said yes but was still annoyed at the fact the questions were being brought up again.

"How long have you been here..?" *Gak paused before looking down, thinking hard. Gak looked over at Ellen with hesitation.*

~THE SECRETS OF ZELPHA~

"I... I... can't answer that question." He held back and said nothing more. Well, that certainly hadn't helped Ellen's curiosity. It might have just made it worse. The stern expression had returned,

"No more questions." He instructed her. Now apologetic, Ellen realised she had reached the gate of the library. Due to the time, it's locked by bars until Gak grabbed another crystal-like object and it opened.

"You're lucky I'm the one who found you," He stated.

"Trust me, you don't know how thankful I am." She replied, wanting to get inside to find James.

"Just find James in there and get to bed soon, and I mean soon. The student dorms are straight ahead; have a good night." Gak walked off as Ellen looked in the direction of the library. As she walked in she saw someone sitting towards the back. It's James. With his nose in a book. She shouted his name, causing him to instantly look up at her startled.

"What are you doing here? We need to leave, now; or we're both going to get in trouble—" she was cut off by James when he told her to stop talking, ignoring him, she asked.

"Why are you even here—" to get cut off again. His voice was stern, making Ellen even more worried than before.

"—This place is dangerous, you need to stop being so reckless." She looked at him like he was crazy.

"Are you kidding me right now?" She asked. James responded,

~THE SECRETS OF ZELPHA~

"Haven't you noticed how much magic this place has?" Ellen continued to look at James worriedly, still questioning his seriousness. She wandered off a bit until she looked James- dead in the eye, and answered.

"Everyone keeps saying that." And had added a bit of insecurity at the end.

"Magic isn't real!" James looked at her, he thought about how he could say this the best. After he made his decision, he looked at Ellen drastically, he said to her

"It is!" This took a toll on Ellen, but James continued.

"You can'' live in denial forever." James took Ellen's hand giving her a trusting look and said.

"Listen to me, if anyone finds out that we don't have magic, we're goners." Ellen looked at James shocked, the worried feeling began to pile on even more now. It took a while for her to understand but then she suddenly said,

"What?! James! But what about going home?" James hesitated a bit. He released his grip on Ellen's hand but still looked at her with a stern expression, and tried to beat the reality into her mind.

"This world is dangerous! It doesn't work like yours." James paused for a moment when he realised that he had chosen the wrong words. He quickly looked away from Ellen. "I mean, ours... how our world works."

Ellen's reaction was instant - she began to gain awareness and understanding as to what was happening in the world around her. She sat down feeling somewhat a speck of suspicion around James and acted more seriously.

"You're acting weirder than usual. Are you ok?" This caused James to look her back in the eyes.

"Why are you so paranoid, James? Everyone here seems fairly nice!" James looked away again, in thought about how much Ellen cared about him, he got up and hugged her. He pulled away and looked at her urgently then he placed his hands on her shoulders.

"Don't let them deceive you, you must stay alert." He put an even more cautious tone on this time but a hint of seriousness was still there, and he continued. "Pay attention to your surroundings, pay attention to what the teachers say."

Ellen looked at him with worry and confusion. Her mind was thinking about what just happened, but one thing was for sure. She looked at James with a sense of urgency.

"Do you have a fever? Should I take you to a nurse or something-" But James suddenly cut her off.

"NO!" His response caused Ellen to jump in surprise then looked at James with a confused and scared expression.

Upset that he startled Ellen, he made up a quick excuse. "No. Sorry. Just… tired." He constantly hesitated to show he wasn't truly tired and that something was happening. He sighed.

"Look, you need to promise me you won't tell anyone that you don't have magic." Ellen hesitates for a moment.

~THE SECRETS OF ZELPHA~

"Promise me." He got more and more stern throughout his sentence.

Ellen decided to make her brother happy so she had no choice but to nod "A- alright, I promise." Satisfied with her answer, James suddenly got a fuzzy feeling all over his body then turned out of Ellen's view and looked at his hand.

What is he looking at? Ellen asked herself. Under his breath, he kept a mental note. *They have no time left and they need to finish this one up. Quickly!*

"We're running out of time." he blurted out loud. Now swiftly he turned back to Ellen with a calm look but there was now a sense of panic and haste roaming around them.

"Ellen, I need you to trust me. Okay?" James urged.

A trusting relationship between siblings felt important to both of the children, however - she most certainly wasn't ready to trust him. Even though James - being her brother - there was something about him that made her want to be alert.

"Give me one good reason why I should trust you when you're acting like a crazy person—" Knowing he had no other choice James shoved the book he was reading into Ellen's hand, *it'll be the quickest way for her to understand* he thought.

"Read this page. Now," he instructed. She told him that they had to leave, they would get in trouble if they were found out of the dorms at this time.

"Please," he said in an urgent tone. Sighing, she took a seat on the floor next to him and began reading.

~THE SECRETS OF ZELPHA~

"'After the school was built, the worlds were at peace for another century. The school did wonders and had even begun expanding to allow non-magical students in.'" she read aloud, her head instinctively turned to face him. "See, James? They allowed non-magical people in!" she explained, James' panic still didn't make sense to her. "I don't know why you're making me read thi-"

"-Just keep reading; and quick!" James interrupted her, "We need to hurry." Ellen looked at him, trying to decide whether it was worth her time to read it or not. After she saw the desperation on his face, though, she decided to keep going.

"'Tension grew between each universe and eventually, they all drew away from the school. It wasn't until thousands of years later that the school mysteriously reopened again; but this time, non-magical beings would not be attending since they were now deemed as dangerous and a threat to everyone. There have been reported cases of non-magical beings attending the school, all at different times and all in a single "team" as the school calls them. Officials say that the specific "team" information is private and will not be available or accessible to anyone. All that can be said is that the non-magical beings have been handled and thrown into the most secure jail in the universe. Turn to Page 58 for more information on 'The Jail'." Before her brain could even process everything that she had read, James quickly snatched the book out of her hands, turning it at exactly page 58. "Jesus! Why

~THE SECRETS OF ZELPHA~

are you so?-" She asked but didn't even get an answer before James handed her the book back.

"HERE!" he exclaimed.

"Alright..." she sighed. "'The most secure jails are The Deathstone Jails, mostly used to hold all mortal beings found on the planet. The jails are filled with high security and traps for anyone who tries to escape or enter. It is quoted that 'Once the prisoners are there, they stay there.' and that they are supplied with food and water daily, just enough to keep them alive. If any mortal or non-magical being is found, they must be handed in. Those who hide them, protect them, cover them and help them will also be thrown in the jails with them.'" For a second, she felt as if her eyes only scanned the page, leaving her confused. Suddenly, she started feeling overwhelmed, as the information was settling in. "I-I'm sorry, I can't read anymore... it's too much."

Grabbing the book back, James ripped out the page and shoved it into her shaky hands. She was unsure what to do with it, and as soon as James picked up on that, he looked her in the eye.

"Here, put this in your pocket. Whatever you do, don't lose it. Don't let anyone see it. Trust me when I say you'll thank me later!"

"Thank you?!" Ellen started. "We're literally going to die if anyone finds out!"

~THE SECRETS OF ZELPHA~

"-Which is a perfect reason not to tell anyone about our lack of magic!". The two were suddenly startled by the library door unlocking. James grabbed Ellen's hand out of habit, dragging her off her seat and towards the exit. Ellen quickly fastened her pace, due to her panic. It turned out that the one who startled them was Ms Gaunt. She walked into the library, quickly noticing the book on the floor. Annoyed by what she thought was the irresponsibility of the people who left it there, she picked up the book, let out another annoyed shrug, and tucked it away in a jacket.

"Hopefully... no one saw us.." Ellen muttered, taking a few deep breaths in. "Never... again. I'm never doing this again.."

James looked at her, sadness flashed across his face. Suddenly, James's appearance flickered from James to a girl Ellen couldn't recognize. As they were both running, exhausted, Ellen couldn't figure out any of her characteristics. "W-who..." she stuttered before finishing her sentence. "Who are you?!"

"You'll meet me soon enough, Ellen." A combination of their voices responded, "I'm counting on you." Ellen just continued to run with her, as though she had no control over her body, like it was not her own, "We all are."

~ 4 ~

TIME TO PREPARE

A mortified Nyx wailed in what seemed to be mental pain.

"WAKE UP!! GET YOUR BUTTS OUT OF BED, QUICKLY!" he looked at Ellen, now half awake, and James who was still sleeping like a baby, and screamed

"—WE'RE LATEEEE!!! GET UP! WE NEED TO HURRY, WE'VE PRACTICALLY ALREADY MISSED BREAKFAST!" James shot up responding with a scream "WHAT?! NOT BREAKFAST?!"

James and Nyx rush around while Ellen drags herself out of bed, wanting the chaos to end. Finally, she had enough energy to form a few words "Ugh... last night was so... weird. Promise me that you won't do that again James..." The two frantic children looked at each other in confusion until Nyx burst out with "She's probably talking about your snoring." With a disgusted look stuck to his face all you could hear was "HEY! I

~THE SECRETS OF ZELPHA~

don't snore! *You're* the one who *SNORES!*" from James in response until he tried to make himself seem smart by continuing with "I'm a sophisticated young man after all."

Both of the students sniggered, Nyx then brought the topic back to breakfast while dragging them out of the dorm room.

"It's 8:50 am, we have ten minutes to hopefully get something to eat and then get to Zelpha Hall."

Knowing they had to hurry to keep James and his stomach happy they start to run, Ellen slowly dragging behind.

"Uh, YEAH we better hurry! I need food, NOW!"

They finally reach the cafeteria door, and as he came to a halt Nyx fell to the ground screaming "WE'RE HERE" whilst making an absolute fool out of himself. The three looked at the blue team as all of the other students went back to their food indifferent to Nyx's fall. Scrambling up off the floor, the three head over to yellow team who have a table with three seats spare. Nyx flopped onto the chair, clearly still in pain but more focused on the food.

"How was that fall," Dusk asked, a bit concerned but entertained by it.

"Looked like it hurt" she followed up with. Unbothered by the fall Nyx turned to Coverly.

" Don't tell us that we–"

"--missed breakfast? Ok, I won't," she responded.

Gale looked at them and laughed. "Geez, guys! You're twenty minutes late!"

~THE SECRETS OF ZELPHA~

He grabbed his fork, picked up some food, and ate. James glared at the laughing boy and grabbed his silverware.

"Give me some of that!" without a blink, James stabbed some of Gale's food and shoved it into his mouth. Dusk facepalmed at the action while the other two stared at them.

"Hey! That's mine!" Gale yelled in frustration at James.

"Not anymore," James responded with a mouth full of food. He surrendered at James' actions Gale just sighed and muttered to himself.

"I guess some things never change." Nyx looked at him while he sat down next to Coverly.

"What do you mean by that?" questioned Nyx.

Gale and Coverly looked at Nyx and then at each other - realising that they had forgotten that Nyx and Ellen were new. Coverly stifled a small giggle while Gale answered.

"Last year whenever James was late he always ate my food" Gale glared at James, meanwhile James continued to eat - ignoring him.

"Sharing is caring, my friend" she sang at Gale, with a smirk as he levelled her with a glare. Gale sighed and then decided to play along with her tone.

"True" Gale nodded his head. James smirked as he shoved more food from Gale's plate into his mouth without Gale noticing.

"So technically, I've never missed a meal at school in my life" James stuck his tongue out at Gale.

~THE SECRETS OF ZELPHA~

"Thanks to me" Gale pointedly looked at James with a smirk.

"Thanks for the food" James replied.

Dusk sighed and turned towards Ellen, ignoring the two guys.

"Well, you look like you didn't sleep at all last night," she said concerned, to Ellen. Ellen looked worn out, with dark circles under her eyes. As she tried to stand near them her head was nodding. James noticed as well and was also concerned for his sister.

"I don't think I did" was her quiet response, fatigue showing hard in her tone.

Unconcerned, Nyx responded to Dusk "I slept like a baby last night. Don't think I've ever slept so well in my life, considering the current state of our room" he said with a mouth full of food. Ellen groaned at Nyx's manners as she sat down next to Dusk. Dusk and James made a slight face of disgust at Nyx before turning back to eating.

"Well, I'm glad one of us got some sleep" Ellen sarcastically said to Nyx.

"You know, you should probably eat something. You're gonna need some energy for today." Dusk told Ellen, her eyebrows furrowed and a small frown on her lips. James, sneakily glanced at the two while still eating. Gale was just trying to enjoy his food.

"Alright," Ellen yawned before grabbing some food for herself.

~THE SECRETS OF ZELPHA~

Gale slammed his hand on the table "James! Don't eat all of it!" James just ignored Gale and kept on eating.

"I'm hungry, leave me alone! You've already had plenty!" It was a shoving contest between the two boys. The other three sighed and ignored them, Nyx just kept on eating.

"I swear, having to deal with you two bickering constantly is like babysitting" Coverly muttered while pointedly looking at Gale and James. A sudden shrill noise sounded before a familiar voice was heard.

"Good morning students. You have five minutes until we require your presence in Zelpha Hall. The teachers have a few announcements before we lead you out to where the first practice trial will be held. I repeat you have five minutes until we require your presence in Zelpha Hall." The voice boomed over the speakers before cutting off as she ended the announcement.

The monitor made a noise as the microphone was turned off. The monitor beeped a pretty funny sound. The announcement was over. It took Ellen back to her childhood, the happy sound of something she can't quite remember. Blue team and yellow team looked at each other, concerned about what was just said. With locked eye contact, they ate a bit faster, while Ellen still didn't eat. Dusk looked at her worried.

"You better eat something before you run out of time" Ellen looked back at her and got a sandwich. She puts it in her mouth nervously, afraid of what will happen with the magical food. Until

~THE SECRETS OF ZELPHA~

"Woah! This is actually really good!" Dusk laughed at her, happy to see her enjoy it. She grabbed her sandwich and waved it around excitedly.

"Yeah, they make the best breakfasts here. Pretty sure it's to bribe everyone to get up early." Nyx looked over at Dusk, exclaiming happily with a ton of food in her mouth

" I love it here already; the food won me over!" James looked at her and thought about the food. Until he realized that that was the idea.

"You and me both".

Coverly looked at Nyx, who put even more food in his mouth. As he tried to say something, he almost gags. Coverly starts laughing on Nyx's back.

"Calm down, you don't want to make yourself sick!" Nyx, who stopped coughing, looked at them, suddenly having an idea:

"Speaking of sickness, is it possible to get away with not doing the Trial Game today?" Dusk looked at Nyx, a little troubled.

" Umm... I'm not sure about that."

Ellen was a little happier because of the food. She was actually looking forward to the day and asked excitedly

"What are we doing today anyways?"

Gale was very nonchalant and bored with the question, he didn't think it was a big deal. It's something they do every year!

~THE SECRETS OF ZELPHA~

"It's just a stupid exercise where they gather all the first years up and make them present their talent."

Ellen lays her sandwich down, a little scared by the answer. *This wouldn't mean they had to use magic right?* She cuts out and finally gets enough courage to ask

"Talent...?" Coverly tries to correct her statement of Gale, as he tries to make the situation better. What she didn't know was that she just made the situation worse.

"What kind of magic they have." Ellen and Nyx are shocked, this couldn't be true! Gale turned to James and exclaimed excitedly to him.

"Gosh, FINALLY!" After that he said a lot softer, hoping nobody heard him. That of course didn't work.

"I swear, I really gotta put my foot down this year..." Suddenly he notices the table looking at him. So he turned fast to James.

"From now on if you're late to a meal, I choose how much food you take from me." Nyx looked at them like they were crazy, and continued to try and talk herself out of the Trail Game. The nervousness in her voice was clear, but only if you listened closely.

"Why do we need to show everyone? That's just unnecessary."
Sadly for Nyx, Dusk was great at hearing emotions in voices. She tried to comfort Nyx, still in thought that he had powers.

~THE SECRETS OF ZELPHA~

"I think it's a health and safety thing. You know since we obviously aren't allowed to use our magic to hurt other people except for when we're in The Games." Once Gale had finished his conversation with James, he thought it was a good idea to join this one.

"My parents forbid me from using magic."
Coverly lit up, something she isn't alone in! "My parents don't like it when I use my magic either. But they can't rule me forever." but Gale still missed something, until he had it!

" Yeah. What magic do you guys have anyways?"

This made Ellen very uncomfortable, she panicked and tried to say something. " Umm—" Luckily, Nyx noticed what was going on- so he quickly helped with " —It's, uhm, kind of boring." Coverly still wanted to know what magic they had, since it was something pretty important. Magic was just a part of everyone and everything, so it was commonplace to know other people's magic. So she tried to comfort them, partially to make them come out of their shell and socialise; partially because she was also curious.

"Nah, I'm sure it's cool!"
Until she slowly stopped herself after noticing how pale Ellen was to ask if she was okay.

"I-I'm fine, just a little nervous about The Games"
Not wanting there to be an awkward silence, giving away their lack of powers, Nyx quickly asked "Anyways, what kind of magic

~THE SECRETS OF ZELPHA~

do you and Gale have?" excitedly, Coverly turned to focus on James.

"I'll show you..." her sage green eyes slowly faded to an off-white.

Then suddenly they began to glow. While her eyes glowed white, she lightly shook, seeming to strain herself. Suddenly the straining stopped, she seemed completely comfortable, but still glowing eyes looking at James. Then the young boy started to levitate, no more than three feet above his chair. James visibly did not find this funny, scared of heights

"Ahaha... alright, Coves. That's enough showing off. Put me down now."

Laughing his but off as he saw how scared James was, Nyx banged on the table

"WOAH! THAT'S AWESOME!!" Everyone started giggling. James looked at them irritated and tried to sound less scared and more stern.

"Did you even hear me?" Coverly waved her hands a bit. That made James float even higher.

"Coves?!"

James was now screaming in fear. "Make him spin! Make him spin!" James gets very annoyed by the childlike behaviour of his friends.

"Listen to me!!"

~THE SECRETS OF ZELPHA~

Ellen was amazed by James floating in the sky, he kicked around and tried to fly with his head up. Ellen just looked at him laughing
"Sick!"
James was now absolutely losing it, kicking around trying to swim down as an astronaut in space. Sadly for James, this had no effect
"COVES! PUT ME-"
Coverly saw a great opportunity now his head was down. She let her eyes stop glowing. James screamed and suddenly crashed down on the floor.
"Ouch."
Not in much pain, nobody comments on the 'ouch'. Nyx though was still pretty curious. "Now, what about you Gale?" Gale looked pretty uncomfortable but still closed his eyes. Suddenly some smoke appears and in a few seconds, Gale isn't there anymore, but a wolf! James loves the wolf. Ellen gasped and petted Gale. Suddenly James had an idea
"DO A BEE! DO A BEE!!" The smoke was there again, and there was Gale. He glared at James with an 'are you kidding me?' look. James nodded his head with a yes. Gale rolled his eyes, looked at James, and focused hard. So hard that you see the dimples on Gale's face. And there's a bee!
"SAY THE THING, SAY THE THING!!" James squealed at the top of his lungs, gaining more attention than

~THE SECRETS OF ZELPHA~

what he already had from his fall. Gale sighed, he seemed as though he most definitely wasn't ready for James' reaction.

"Bzz Bzz"

"YESSSS!" he screamed even louder than before. Embarrassed by his friend, Gale commented,

"You're lucky I can't sting you, otherwise I'd die." Not wanting an argument, and as a girl who seemed to have been the mother of these two for a long time, Coverly said "And we don't want that, *do we, boys?*" While Gale turned back to his human form Dusk told them that the group should go to the hall, so they're not late. Blue and yellow team stood up, as they left and the table magically cleared.

James tried to put some fun into the conversation. Hyping them up "Today's gonna be pretty easy, for me and the yellow team at least, we have this solid." Ellen looked over, confused about what James was saying. "It's gonna be fine for you guys too, you're nice enough. I'm sure the teachers will swoon over your magical kindness." Ellen was sure that James was joking with her, laughing at him. James gave her a reassuring look.

"Are you being sarcastic with me?" said Ellen laughing at James.

Nyx giggled, at her remark. "No need to sucker up, aye James?" caught red-handed, James ventured further in on the joking part. "I'm sure we'll make *loads* of new friends. I'm so popular, *everyone* wants to be friends with me!" Ellen starts to

~THE SECRETS OF ZELPHA~

laugh at his 'popular' joke. "Then you better get going, 'Mr. Popular'. " fitting the kind of conversation they're having." Of course, I'm sure my dear friend Gale misses me. It's not like I saw him less than a minute ago. I'll see you guys later." after saying that James walked away. Ellen and Nyx laughed as he walked away because he whipped his hips and was pretending to be popular, even if people found it very weird. While Nyx was still laughing, Ellen's facial expression changed. When he noticed that, he looked at Ellen.

"I'm kinda nervous. Dunno how these 'Practice Trial Games' work. Let's just stick together and hope for the best." Ellen said when she noticed Nyx looking. Nyx laughed at her proposal "That's how I always do things. Stick with a friend, cry together, and hope things work out." A boy in a brown and grey uniform walked over to Ellen and Nyx, he had black hair with dark grey stripes in them. His uniform suited his eyes, which were grey too. He also wore black trainers.

"Hey! I'm Thrust, it's nice to meet you. I'm in the brown team by the way if you can't tell from the uniform, haha! I hope we can get to know each other better, even if we are going against each other in the long run." The boy said introducing himself.

Feeling uncomfortable, Ellen responded with a quick "Yeah, it's nice to meet you too" comment. Leaving the rest of the conversation to Nyx, who was looking down at the boy's shoes. Looking back up at his face he asked "Where'd you get the uniform?" The boy looked down "Oh, this?" with a little kick of

~THE SECRETS OF ZELPHA~

the leg, looking down at his uniform. "I had it last year; I thought I should keep it for this year too. I don't even want to think about getting a uniform that used to be owned by a non-magical being. Well, it seems as though I have to go, see ya!" The boy started to walk away, with a bit of a skip mixed in with his usual walk. Ellen's initial thoughts were *he'd kept the same uniform for that long, yuck!*

"I don't trust him." She followed that up by asking

"And why is everyone so... weird and against non-magical people? What did we even do?" Suddenly a bell rang and Ms Gaunt called for everyone's attention.

"SILENCE! Thank you. Now, I know that the new students don't know what happens today as they seem to know nothing."

Ellen shot a dirty look at Ms Gaunt, for the rude comment.

"So, I shall pass you over to Mr Gallo, who will explain to you all about how today was going to go down." A man walked onto the stage, and all students - besides Ellen and Nyx - stood in respect of the teacher entering the stage. Suddenly, James drags Ellen up. Not wanting to seem rude, Nyx shot up.

"Thank you, everyone, you may sit." All of the students sat down at the same time, followed by Ellen and Nyx.

"It is great to finally meet you all. I'm sure this will be a great year, I love seeing new and fresh faces here at this wonderful place. Don't stress out students - the other teachers and I will guide you today and help you with anything. Today though, we will be sorting your uniforms. But just to clarify the most important rule today: Students will NOT use their magical powers on other students or members of staff, to cause harm. There are severe punishments if anyone is caught breaking this rule. I will now select a few teams at a time to go up and get changed into their uniform. All of the uniforms have a magical charm cast onto them so they won't get dirty; therefore, you will wear them all year round." Ellen thought *oh, so that's why Thrust was still wearing his. Unhygienic nonetheless.*

"That includes during your training for The Games, your magic classes, history classes, and for when you enter The Games. When your team is selected, please go up the staircase on the student side and to the fitting room to collect your clothes. Your team leader will show you the way. Let's start with blue team. The rest of you may talk amongst yourselves. Blue team, you may stand."

James once again dragged Ellen and Nyx up from their seats. Ms Gaunt ushered them out of the room demanding they be as quick as possible. Needing to get out - Ellen and Nyx rushed out of the room, followed by James and Miss Yonda, they all headed up the staircase Mr Gallo mentioned. Stood side by side, James asked Miss Yonda

"Miss Yonda! You worked for the yellow team last year, right?" Nodding her head she realizes and stated that he's friends with a few members of the team. Ellen quickly turned around, followed by Nyx asked,

~THE SECRETS OF ZELPHA~

"Wait, so you were with Dusk, Coverly, and Gale?" Nyx continued with "You used to be their teacher? That's awesome!" Happy that her group had made friends with students she knew were nice. Miss Yonda called the yellow team sweet and expressed her happiness.

"It just seems like there are so many people to meet! Like, this place is packed!" Ellen observed. The four of them reached the entryway of the changing room.

"Here we are! Be quick, you lot; the other teams will be here soon. Just pick a blue team outfit and try it on; the uniform will magically adjust to your perfect size when you wear it. I'll wait out here and let you know when the next team arrives."

The three children walked in, they started to search through clothes, and all looked for something already in their style. There was everything you could imagine: dresses in every colour of the rainbow, jeans, trousers, leggings, hoodies, shirts, t-shirts, and blouses. You name it, you'll find it. James grabbed himself a navy blue jumper, dark grey joggers, and white trainers and headed into the changing room while Ellen and Nyx talked to each other.

"This place is so big, and we haven't even seen everything yet!" Nyx looked around him as he stated this. Ellen sighed as her shoulders sank,

"I know right... I've already gotten lost once." Nyx looked worried at Ellen, he saw that she was exhausted.

~THE SECRETS OF ZELPHA~

"Yeah, what happened last night? You seemed pretty... off this morning" He questioned her, his tone somewhat quiet but forward with his question. Ellen cringed at this, aware she had to tell him about the situation with Myrtle and Gak.

"Well, last night I was looking for James because he wasn't in the dorm room and I got worried. So when I went out looking for him, I bumped into Myrtle who... sort of... managed to get me trapped in a greyed-out area...?" Without thinking about the fact his actions had consequences he instantly raised his voice to shout in Ellen's face

"WHAT?! YOU WENT INTO A GREY-" he was instantly cut off by a whisper-yell.

"SHHHHHH! KEEP YOUR VOICE DOWN! D'YOU WANT THE WHOLE SCHOOL TO HEAR YOU!?" Calming himself down, Nyx took a few deep breaths and started to whisper, asking her questions.

Ellen told him that he must not tell anyone what happened. The information stayed between them. As Nyx asked more, he found out a teacher managed to find out and that she was locked in a greyed-out room.

"You were locked in a ROOM!?" he shouted once again. Disturbed by the uproar, Miss Yonda opened the door just enough to catch a glimpse of the commotion in the room. Miss Yonda asked if they were okay and received a loud response.

"We're fine" Ellen stared at Nyx in a way to express her anger and instructed him to keep his voice down.

~THE SECRETS OF ZELPHA~

"Just let me explain, and *please* don't yell again!—" James then slowly wandered back into the room, his jumper a nice navy blue colour that seemed to radiate comfort and warmth. His joggers were a dark grey with a simple blue stripe - which showed his pride in his team colour. On his feet were a pair of soft white trainers that seemed to fit perfectly with the rest of his attire. Similar to Miss Yonda, the young boy was interested in what the commotion was about, a question he voiced whilst looking at them both, while Ellen began going slightly pale in the face.

"Uh... School!" at the same time that Nyx awkwardly mumbled, "Um... Food". A silence boomed throughout what Ellen felt to be the entire school. She looked them both in the eye, as they tried to come up with an excuse that could get them out of this mess.

"I mean..." she lost her words again. She looked helplessly at Nyx, in the hope he could think of something. Aware he messed up the last time Nyx was afraid to do it again but still said something

"Ahaha, wow! Love the outfit, James! Ahaha..." Suspicious of what was happening with them, James looked the two up and down.

"Thanks, Nyx. Looks like you've got your clothes, why don't you get changed now?"

Nyx looked at Ellen, and James said " I'll keep Ellen company." Nyx was still hesitant but was too embarrassed to go any further

~THE SECRETS OF ZELPHA~

on with the conversation "Umm, a-alright" and walked off, James tried to say something to Ellen, but Nyx heard them. He looked doomful at James and continued to walk.

"So, how are you finding the place? I know it might all be a bit of a shock; it's quite big. You can get lost very easily here…" he continued, to try and get some information out of Ellen, who was still a bit unsure of what to do.

"Yeah," she said nervously. "I still don't know how I got here or what on Earth is going on, but everyone besides the red team and Ms Gaunt seems nice." Looking around anxiously, James quietly agreed and continued to chat.

Nyx finally came out of the changing room in a similar outfit, jet-black jeans with a dark blue hoodie - looking sleeker than James did. After some small talk about Nyx's outfit, James grabbed the door and propped it open with his foot before shoving Ellen through the opening and into the changing room. The door behind Ellen slammed with a loud CLANG! Both Nyx and James burst out laughing as Ellen spoke to them through the door, making her words muffled. She huffed before she quickly got dressed.

After she was done, she heard more voices join in the conversation outside. Intrigued, she checked her outfit in the mirror beside her. She detangled her multicoloured hair with her fingers, like a brush. She continuously adjusted her jumper until it was perfect, as her jeans hugged her waist, climbing down her legs - ending at her ankles. As she fixes her hair, Ellen realises that

~THE SECRETS OF ZELPHA~

she seemed to slowly and steadily settle into the school. It was scary to her, she just wanted to go home - but then she remembered; that she found her brother after being apart for so long, she had always dreamt of the day they would find each other again. Ellen's eyes got blurry with tears, quickly she wiped them away with her sleeve before breathing deeply. *I'm with my brother now. I'm not losing him now... we will get home.* Ellen swung the door open to see Bridget ahead of her.

Bridget's voice could be heard above anyone else's.

"Hello all - the most awesome person ever has entered the room. Yes; hello, hello! It is I, Bridget!" With her final word, she looked around the room expecting applause; the crowd was silent, and she took a bow - making the awkward silence more awkward. The first to break the atmosphere was Ellen.

"Loving the entrance," she commented, leaning against the nearest wall.

It seemed Bridget had a middle parted split-dyed hair - one side tawny with the other dirty blonde, hanging low towards her hips. Soft, peach-coloured skin with rosy cheeks and light greenish hazel eyes gazed at Ellen. A light green bomber jacket rested over a black crop top with matching black shorts. Bridget - 5'8 - stood tall beside Ellen, and looked down at her with a soft smile full of energy.

The two others in the room were Yadira and Reid. Yadira stood beside Bridget, seemingly close to her - like a friend - trying to calm Bridget down. Long black hair covered her brown skin with a fringe that stopped right before her black-coloured eyes. Yadira had an oversized dark green hoodie and clay-coloured jeans.

Although Reid was trying to hide in the background, her bright green jacket stood out against the other two. Although seemingly standing out due to that - when she was in social situations, she rarely contributed much, instead choosing to listen to others and take in and learn about the people she spent most of her time with. Nobody had ever heard her talk above a whisper, but when she did speak, she held the authority of someone beyond her years and status. Soft forest green eyes glanced around the room. Her medium-length onyx hair rested lightly on her tanned skin. Peeking out from her jacket was a white t-shirt and a pleated grey skirt. On her feet were white tennis shoes with long black stockings covering her legs.

A voice from outside the room interrupted the two teams' conversation. It was Miss Yonda.

"Right you three, back downstairs" she called the blue team. The three said their goodbyes to the green team, with hopes of seeing them around the school again.

Ellen was nervous, she was befriending more and more people here when that was not her plan. She needed to focus on getting her and her brother home to safety, and revealing what was truly going on in their Overworld dimension. Nonetheless, she kept up her happy facade as the other students were nice, even if Ellen was not up to making any attachments. While

~THE SECRETS OF ZELPHA~

walking back to Zelpha Hall, the blue team, and Miss Yonda decided to have some small talk.

"So what do you guys think of the green team?" Miss Yonda asked as she heard most of the conversation the teams had. After a short chat about the green team and their outfits, Miss Yonda sent her team back into Zelpha Hall, in a rushed urgent tone,

"Right, quiet for Ms Gaunt. Now, everyone please take a seat on the front row." Anxiously, the three children scurried into the room and sat down as fast as they could, not wanting to upset the lady ahead of them.

Miss Yonda shushed and ushered blue team inside the main hall to hear what the miserable old wretched lady had to say. James then nods and leads Nyx and Ellen to the benches.

"Welcome back blue team. Continue to talk amongst yourselves. Gak to the staff room now... young boy." Ms Gaunt exclaimed in a serious tone, she was not happy and Gak wasn't going to hear the end of it. Gak walked over to the staff room, seeming down, preparing to have his ears talked off by Ms Gaunt.

"Oh no please no..." Ellen looked down and muttered to herself. She really hoped this wasn't about the situation she thought it was about

"What's up?" James asked with a worried look covering his face. He didn't know what Ellen was going on about and he sure didn't have a good feeling about it.

~THE SECRETS OF ZELPHA~

" Ms Gaunt sent Gak to the staff room, I wonder if it's about..." She questioned quietly until Dusk, Coverly, and Gale walked over to the siblings, oblivious to the situation.

"Hey guys!" Coverly shouted excitedly. She headed over to stand behind James.

"Don't worry Ellen... It'll be fine."James whispered to his sister under his breath.

"Hey guys!" He then shouted back, quickly changing his whole emotion and expression.

"Woah someone's a little energetic!" Coverly replied, a little surprised while a small smile appeared at the corner of her mouth. Ms Gaunt walked towards the teams and stood in front of the pink team's teacher.

"Ms. Tilli, lead your group off." She orders with a rare calm tone.

"Yes Ms Gaunt, come on guys!" Ms Tilli encouraged her team

After the pink team leaves, Miss Zana comes in with the green team. After giving a smile to the members of the green team, Ellen finally caught sight of Dusk.

"Hey, Dusk!" Ellen said with a smile on her face.

"Hi, Ellen," Dusk responded with a solemn face and in a monotone voice.

"Dusk. What's up with you? Did anything happen?"Nyx added, worriedly.

~THE SECRETS OF ZELPHA~

"Nothing happened." Dusk blurts out, with the same tone in her voice, not having a care in the world that they were a bit worried.

Everyone looked around for anyone to have an idea about why Dusk was acting like that.

"I know what's up, I'm sorry about it. I found out what the red team is truly like last night. They are horrid." Ellen admitted, disgusted by red team's actions. She didn't understand why Myrtle did that to her, she had only just arrived.

"Finally someone using their brain. Anyway... What did they do this time?" Dusk asks, wondering what happened.

"Well, the 'main gir-" Ellen started until she was cut off by Dusk. She showed clear worry and confusion on her face as she slightly tilted her head to the side.

"Do you mean Myrtle?" Dusk questioned, looking at the girl in front of her.

"Yeah, that girl. Anyway, I was looking for James and she said she would help and sh-" As she continued to explain what happened and why she ended up in a greyed area she was cut off as Myrtle and Laryse made their way over to Ellen, Myrtle had a little smirk in the corner of her mouth. Ellen didn't know what to expect but she didn't have a good feeling about it.

"Hey Ellen... I saw you in a grey area last night; poor thing. But since we're besties, I won't tell anyone. Promise! But if I catch you again I'll have to tell Ms Gaunt." Myrtle mentioned to the whole group, seeming to act quiet but talking loudly to

~THE SECRETS OF ZELPHA~

attract more attention. She had a mischievous grin slapped onto her face, everyone could see, her plan was so obvious, it's like she didn't even try to hide it.

"WHAT!? YOU WERE IN AN OUT-OF-BOUNDS AREA!?" Gale exclaimed, he was shocked and a little angry. From what wasn't covered by his beautiful pink hair, Ellen saw his eyebrows disappear behind his fringe and his eyes widened.

"What were you thinking, you idiot!?" Dusk asked angrily, she was livid and very disappointed in her. She thought out of all people Ellen would be the last person to go to an out-of-bounds area, Dusk thought Ellen was the type of student to follow all of the rules, even the silly ones.

"I can explain!" Ellen shouted, hoping for her friends to hear her out before anything else was said or more people shouted at her. She could feel tears flood her eyes. Ellen didn't understand why Myrtle was out for her, she had only just got here and she was already enemies with people. Myrtle just had to make things hard for her.

"Awww, hey Dusk! How are you and your little friends doing? Keeping them on a tight leash I see; are they your pets now? So we have little miss, I-was-in-a-greyed-area-last-night and the one who likes the colour red. What's their name again Laryse?" Myrtle asked while her grin only grew bigger. She thought of herself as funny but even her little minions Laryse and Evelyn didn't laugh; they just stayed quiet watching it all happen. It was all going the way Myrtle wanted it to and she did not feel a single ounce of guilt about causing trouble between others.

"Nyx..." Laryse mumbled her head pointing to the ground. She just wanted to leave but didn't have the guts to tell Myrtle to move on and leave the innocent people alone and just get on with their day.

"Oh yeah, Nyx. Gotta remember that; it would be SO rude if I forgot." Myrtle chuckled slightly, looking back at Laryse for her reaction but she was still looking at the ground not paying attention to what was going on. Myrtle looked back round her laughing coming to a stop and her facial expression turning more intimidating. Ellen was confused about why Myrtle was acting this way because the group had been minding their own business, she didn't even know Myrtle was in the room.

"Wait, how do you remember our names...?" She questioned, hoping that the pair would leave them alone after the question had been answered. But soon enough she regretted saying anything at all.

"Ellen. Use your brain. Just like Dusk said. Magic... remember? It exists... we all have it" Myrtle pointed out, making her eyes stare into Ellen's soul, hoping she would slip up so she could have more things to use against the innocent girl. Ellen could tell Myrtle was after her and that she wasn't going to stop until she had completely ruined everything for her. It stuck in Ellen's head.

~THE SECRETS OF ZELPHA~

"Magi-" Nyx had a thought and was about to blurt it out but was immediately interrupted by Ellen, who knew whatever he was going to say about magic couldn't be good for them or James. She gave Nyx a look, a sign to stop talking.

"Yes of course I know that I was just a little shocked as that's not what our world's magic does," Ellen said with a smile trying not to seem so suspicious. She couldn't have any more attention, especially from Myrtle. She was already onto Ellen about magic from last night when she couldn't find James. The last thing she wanted was for Myrtle to have more of an advantage over her.

"Yeah, our world doesn't have that." Nyx agreed, playing along with Ellen's plan and hoping the situation would end soon so then everyone could get on with their day and just forget about everything to do with the mean girls of the school. Nyx wasn't keen on Myrtle and Laryse, yes he is jealous that they got red but he'd rather be on a team colour that he didn't like than have to be around them for however long he had to stay in Zelpha.

"Your world sucks... Anyway, who cares?" Laryse muttered looking around the room thinking of an idea for how to escape. She wasn't enjoying this, she didn't understand why Myrtle was like this. Nobody did, maybe Myrtle was just a horrible person or that's how she was raised. She never explained about her actions and why she was like that. It seemed more mysterious than the Zelpha world, which was something.

~THE SECRETS OF ZELPHA~

"Laryse, don't be mean! These guys are our friends, after all, however, it is strange not to have the reading mind's power." Myrtle stated, giving Laryse a dirty look while raising her voice at her trying to get her little minion in line. Afterwards, she turned back to the group with a smile, trying to seem sweet and innocent, hoping the group in front of her would share more with her.

"Uh yeah um—" Ellen stuttered slightly, trying to think of something to say while fidgeting and looking all around the room. She desperately tried to think of something to come back with.

"—Our world is just different." Nyx butted back in, coming to the rescue, while slyly trying to change the subject to something completely different and away from magic. Especially before James arrived he hated talking about magic, mostly because he didn't have it but only Nyx and Ellen knew that. But coincidentally James came over, obviously oblivious to the situation but having a concerned look on his face since Myrtle and Laryse were with them.

"What are you all talking about?" He asked politely standing behind Dusk, trying to be a part of the conversation.

"Magic." Ellen quietly said nervously, looking up at him while picking at her fingernails and preparing for his reaction; which she knew wouldn't be a good one.

"WHAT! Why are you talking about magic to these losers? Come on. We're going," James ordered in a very serious

~THE SECRETS OF ZELPHA~

tone as he stomped off into the hallway with his fists clenched and his eyebrows pointed down.

"Well, we better get going," Ellen said quickly as she got up and speed-walked with Nyx by her side. She gave him a worried look and took some deep breaths to get herself ready for how James would react after finding out they were all talking about magic.

"What the..." Dusk questioned while her eyes followed the trio walking away from her and everyone else. Quite suddenly James' voice could be heard from down the corridor, making her jump a little from the sudden loud noise.

"What was that for?" Nyx asked, slightly annoyed at the fact he couldn't say bye to everyone before leaving.

"I'm sorry James," Ellen muttered as she looked at her feet trying to hide the tears burning her eyes. She was crestfallen about how she disappointed her older brother and made him angry.

"Ellen! What are you doing? I told you not to mention magic, please tell me you told them you have magic, if you didn't you're so dead. No, we would all be dead. What are you thinking, you idiots? You're so stupid. We are going to get sent away to cages and never seen again all because of you!" James shouted angrily, his voice echoing through the walls. He paced in front of Ellen and Nyx while they just stood there with guilt all over their faces. It wasn't their fault though. Myrtle was the one who brought up magic they were just going along with it so they

~THE SECRETS OF ZELPHA~

didn't get exposed and thrown into the jails. James was livid and he made the pair flinch at his every movement. Ellen never saw James angry, it was like Zelpha completely changed him.

"Calm down, what's the issue with all of this magic stuff anyway?" Nyx questioned, confused but still slightly scared of making the situation worse, he could tell Ellen was about to cry but didn't know what else to do than make James turn the anger to him instead of Ellen.

"Did you not listen to a word I just said?" James spat towards Nyx, he was still angry but a lot quieter than before. He realized if he kept shouting people would hear what they were talking about and they would for sure find out that James, Nyx, and Ellen don't have magic. Then it would be his fault, not theirs.

"Stop shouting James," Ellen demanded while sniffing and wiping the tears from her eyes. She had built up the courage to finally say something to her older brother because it was going to get out of hand sooner or later and she didn't need even more drama starting especially between her and James, she couldn't lose him again.

"Well, you were speaking so fast so I couldn't make out a word you were saying," Nyx added, starting to slightly get annoyed with James and how he was acting towards them; like he was the boss of them both.

"Look, I can't deal with this, just tell me if we are okay Ellen," James stated, taking deep breaths to try and calm himself

~THE SECRETS OF ZELPHA~

down. This was way too stressful for him to handle and he found Ellen and Nyx unhelpful about any of it.

"We are fine. I have kept it all under control." Ellen reassured, wiping the tears from her eyes, and getting her breath back to normal. She looked over at Nyx. He just stood there. He seemed confused but also relieved that James had stopped shouting the walls down.

"Good," James said, walking away and muttering things to himself. Ms Gaunt's old horrible voice could be heard from all over. Most students tried to cover their ears from the noise but it wasn't any use. It was too powerful.

"SILENCE!" She paused while glaring at the students waiting for them to find some respect and quiet down so she could continue talking.

"Right, now that you all have your outfits, you will have a practice trial. Gak will make sure each of you are ready at the door and Mr Gallo will lead you out and I will be behind" Ms Gaunt informed, her voice more controlled than before since the students finally started to listen and stop talking. Sometimes she hated the students, but she could see greatness within them.

"Right, bench by bench please." Mr Gallo ordered, the crowd of students immediately stood up and made their way to the doors, Gak quickly scurried over to let them out without any injuries.

~5~

SHALL WE START?

Mr Gallo approached the students as Gak frantically tried to open the door for all the students to head to the practice grounds. He smiled and waved at Gak, trying to calm the poor young teacher. It seemed to work, as Mr Gallo saw Gak's shoulders loosen at the sight of the older gentleman. The older teacher walked closer to them to help Gak escort the students outside.

"Hello, Gak!" Mr Gallo said.

"Good afternoon, sir!" Gak stated with a stress-filled grin. After stating their greetings, Mr Gallo continued walking past Gak and towards the students. He looked at their faces and saw many different emotions within them. Many are filled with excitement and some are more filled with worry. The teacher sighed and knew he had to calm some students down. Mr Gallo's eyes pondered over the distinctive blue-coloured clothes and saw that James was extremely nervous; his whole body language

~THE SECRETS OF ZELPHA~

screamed distress and anxiety. Placing a hand on James' shoulder, Mr Gallo asked James if he was okay; receiving a smile and a nod, answering the teacher with a positive but strenuous tone of voice. The older teacher nodded and continued walking past the blue team. Gak spoke up as the older gentleman was out of view.

"Okay, off ya go then," Gak said while finally opening the door.

James placed a hand on the backs of Nyx and Ellen, slightly nudging them in front of him. He laughed as Nyx slightly stumbled - responding with a small but friendly glare. Ellen sighed at the two boys but grinned. She wanted to get outside and have a look at what the practice grounds were like.

"Come on guys!" James smirked at the two, even after nudging them to be in front of him- James rushed to be first.

Ellen rolled her eyes at her brother's attitude before walking closer to the door behind Nyx. Suddenly, a hand stopped her from going forward. She slightly jumped back and looked up, seeing the hand belonging to Gak. Ellen was confused about why but did not voice it at the moment.

" Sorry, I need to check you," Gak coughed into his hand.

"Oh, right sir- I understand" Ellen nodded as she tensed her back.

Ellen's mind raced as she heard Gak ask her to empty her pockets. One by one, small items left her pockets and into Gak's hand. Her eyes widened with fear as she felt a specific piece of paper in her grasp. Gak questioned on the paper, his voice was

~THE SECRETS OF ZELPHA~

stern towards Ellen. She fumbled with her words, trying to get her story correct and not to reveal what was written. *Oh my gosh, it's a page from the book he can't see that!* In her panic, she looked at James, trying to get him to help her. Ellen saw the confusion on his face.

"Ellen, what are you waiting for?" James questioned her.

"O-oh, nothing, Gak just needs t-"

"Paper please Ellen." Gak interrupted her

Begrudgingly, Ellen handed over the paper that she was trying to hide. Gak rolled his eyes at her hesitance and opened up the folded paper. Meanwhile, Ellen wrung her hands looking back and forth between the piece of paper and Gak's face. Her thoughts were going a mile a minute with worry. She closed her eyes, wincing at hearing Gak sigh.

"Why are you so worried? It's blank... go ahead" Gak slowly gave the paper back to Ellen.

Opening her eyes, she looked at Gak with shock... the paper the last time she looked at had multiple paragraphs of words - but now according to Gak... it was blank. With it now back in her hands, she shoved it into her pocket, walking away and toward the others. *Oh my... what happened? Maybe it's magic?* Ellen thought to herself as she got closer to her brother and friend.

Each team was searched for items that were deemed prohibited. Only a few students grumbled at some of their stuff being confiscated. Ellen heard Dusk snigger at one of the purple

~THE SECRETS OF ZELPHA~

team members having a meltdown at an item now in Gak's hand. After a few minutes, each team was outside an entrance of what seemed to be a giant castle. Behind her and the others, Ms Gaunt walked closer to Gak. Staring down at the younger teacher, it looked like she was glaring down at him.

"Gak, go." she glowered at him.

"Oh uh, yeah... I mean... yes, Ms Gaunt" Glancing down, Gak walked away.

Mr Gallo walked to the front of the groups and clapped his hands, trying to quiet down all the chit-chat from the students talking with each other.

"Okay, everyone! This is the castle, do not touch anything, or there will be severe consequences- we are not too far now." He spoke loudly, making some students who were right in front of him wince at his volume.

He continued walking forward, signalling the students to follow him as he gave a tour around the castle. Some students started complaining to their friends and teammates about all the stairs and how long they had been walking. Ellen heard complaints even coming from her friends.

"Ugh, my feet hurt!" Nyx whined, annoying James.

"You said that up the stairs," he grumbled back at Nyx. Nyx decided to talk back to James, finding an outlet for boredom.

"Because it's true!" Nyx sassed back. James sighed loudly at this and just ignored him.

~THE SECRETS OF ZELPHA~

"Just give it a rest will you." Rolling his eyes, James responded.
James turned his head to check on Ellen, who had been surprisingly quiet throughout the whole tour so far. He noticed that she was not next to him but slightly away from the group, James frantically looked around and saw her - her face plastered onto the glass of an aquarium. He facepalmed before rushing over to her.

"Ellen! Be careful!" He quietly shouted, standing next to her.

Ellen's face was plastered onto the glass of the aquarium, and a huge smile was on her face. James sighed at her but had a small smile on his face too.
The fish swam frantically around the tank, clearly surprised by her sudden visit and trying to escape. James stared in sympathy for the fish, before sighing. Ellen finally pulled away from the glass to look at James.

"Okay, okay! But there are fishies!" James grabbed Ellen's wrist and dragged her away from the tank, Rolling his eyes in a mix of amusement and exasperation.

"Come on, get back over here" Ellen pulled away from James, Stumbling and then standing without him. Before stopping and looking back to the tank and giving a small wave. As he turned back around he caught Ellen waving at the fish, his smile faded before he grabbed her once more, dragging her towards Nyx. Mr Gallo turned around, all the voices and noise drowning him out.

"Now." but his words fell on deaf ears as no one even looked his way. He gave an irritated sigh, and Ms Gaunt lost her temper.

"SILENCE!!" she shouted in command, as the students spun around to give her their attention. She continued with an enraged speech.

"How dare you talk over another member of staff! I understand this may not be exciting to you at all; Particularly the blue team, but that does NOT give you the right to be disrespectful." The crowd stayed quiet, most likely in fear, as she spoke back up.

"Sorry sir. You may continue." Mr Gallo nodded and began his speech

"Thank you, Ms Gaunt, now as I was saying here is the front gate to the castle. You must NOT leave the paths, the surrounding area of the castle may be seen as dangerous. Now please stay in your respective groups and don't forget to stick to the path!" As the blue team caught Coverly's eye, he got the girls to catch up to them - in an attempt to escape the red team.

"I am so glad we caught up to you, we were stuck with the red team bickering at each other" Coverly panted in exhaustion. Gale, who was most certainly not in the mood for running finally reached the group - strutting up to the arms folded.

~THE SECRETS OF ZELPHA~

"Ugh! Do they ever shut up?" Ellen responded - exhausted from the thought of their situation. The yellow team cried out a no, as Ellen swiftly changed the topic from them.

"Anyways what happens in these Games?" she asked, curiously.

"Well... it's all magic-based..." James hesitated. He gave his teammates a reassuring look yet it didn't seem to affect Nyx's state of mind.

"Excuse me, what did you just say?" Nyx glared at James who had an awkward look on his face.

"It's okay though, I know you two aren't really strong with magic yet but these people will help!" James gave a comforting look to Ellen and Nyx as he tried to reassure them once again.

"Yeah so... uhm... This place must be really old." Ellen looked around the place they all were in before looking at Gale.

"It's actually very old, but what made you say that?" Gale questioned the girl ahead of him.

"I mean... look at these trees! They look ancient!" Ellen stumbled upon her words.

Nyx began to examine the trees around him. Vines and leaves hung from the branches that were covered in crystals and mushrooms. Some of the mushrooms were bigger than Nyx himself. Small talk continued onward about how pretty the trees were - until something caught Ellen's attention. She immediately

~THE SECRETS OF ZELPHA~

lost interest when she heard a scraping sound seemingly coming from the distance,

"Hey, do you guys know what's making that strange sound?" Ellen asked curiously.

"No idea, probably someone in the village," Dusk added to the conversation. Ellen didn't know what was going on, and neither did she care. She wanted to know what this 'village' was.

"Wait- Village? What village?!" she quickly asked - hoping these village folk would know an escape from Zelpha. Ellen's mind was whizzing - the friends she'd make, the home she'd reach.

"Nobody really knows, every time we have a Game it's repeated to us that this place is dangerous and we're never told why, people made conspiracy theories and that's what stuck." Although Ellen didn't know if the village was true, she didn't let that deflate the thought of going home, Chester.

"Wow, that's so weird" she added, looking towards the forest ahead.

The mossy path was encased with a thick forest of trees on either side. The forest began to entice Ellen in, with a warm welcome. Curiosity had beaten her. Shimmering purple crystals grew from the trees, and peaked from the grass - that could barely be seen through the leaves. Vines and leaves filled the forest ahead, and patches of flowers ranging from red, blue and yellow littered the forest floor - creating contrast within the grass below. Large speckled mushrooms and fungi grew from the moss

~THE SECRETS OF ZELPHA~

below her, spotted among the trees, strange in size compared to the forest it resided in - showing the glory of what seemed to be an ancient forest floor. All of a sudden a rustling sound from the leaves below caught all the students' attention.

"Ellen, are you okay?" James asked, worried about his sister. She was staring into the forest, its magic was dragging her in. Taking over her thoughts and words.

"Yeah, what are you on about? We can just go in and check right" The girl's eyes continued to stare dead on at the forest ahead, as it began to engulf her. All five of the other students just stared at each other - lost. Coverly huffed, clearly annoyed at their lack of care towards Ellen's safety - she reached over and grabbed Ellen, dragging Ellen away from the forest. She put an arm over her shoulder, walking with her.

The students made their way along a dirt path with bits of gravel intertwined in the path. They made it to the area where The Games would take place. Surrounding it was a stone-brick wall. The wall was infested and covered with moss and cracks. Standing tall, the wall towered over the students and teachers as they walked towards the mossy archway. Leaves, flowers, and grass consumed it. The area inside had ten stands, one for each colour - seats for each student and teacher, soft coloured carpet and banners; all representing the colours of the teams. Ellen remembered seeing those banners in the dorm rooms. In the air were coloured particles, sparkling and flickering around - like magic.

~THE SECRETS OF ZELPHA~

Mr Gallo walked along the rows of stands and instructed all students to get to their places as he explained The Games. Myrtle started twirling her hair in her fingers, walking towards Gak confidently with each step. She softened her facial expression as she reached him.

"Hey Gak" she giggled flirtatiously.

Gak hid even deeper in his hair as he was most certainly not in the mood to deal with Myrtle and her stupid ideas. He simply responded with her name and asked her to go to her stand. Her response to Gak giving an unamused tone was,

"What's up with you? You don't seem like my normal Gak." she wandered off. He continued to greet each student as they walked past, pointing and waving in the direction of their team stand. All of a sudden Laryse walked over to Ellen

"What do you want, Laryse?" Ellen mumbled.

"We aren't friends? I see how it is." As she turned to have her back facing Ellen, she knocked her over - causing Ellen to stumble. "I really wanted to be your friend but clearly you're an evil little girl, I will have everyone on my side. After all, you're BLUE TEAM" she wickedly stated; finding herself hysterical. Ellen didn't care, she turned her back and saw Dusk trying to speak to Evelyn. *Evelyn's on the red team, why is Dusk speaking to one of THEM?* Ellen wondered. Whilst scanning over the situation she saw that Evelyn was once again not responding. *What is it with that girl?* All of a sudden, each student's conversation came to an abrupt end and Ms Gaunt screamed.

~THE SECRETS OF ZELPHA~

"Silence! Allow Mr Gallo to speak!" Mr Gallo sighed at the sound of Ms Gaunt's sharp voice and quickly moved on.

"Right, thank you, Ms Gaunt! Here is where the Practice Games will take place! The winning team will have their best-performing member spend a whole week in the castle when not in a game! That person will be monitored by Gak and a housekeeper of the castle so NO sneaky business! Everyone find your groups and teachers as The Games are about to begin!"

Out of the corner of Ellen's eye, she could see James pushing and running through the crowd of students to reach Miss Yonda. Now exhausted; James had finally managed to get the teacher's attention. Miss Yonda - who could see distress within him - swiftly tried to calm James down.

"Goodness James! Calm down. Now, what's the matter?" James started to ask about the castle - further leading onto its library. *He's such a nerd* Ellen thought; causing a slight giggle to slip out of her mouth. After Miss Yonda walked over to another teacher, James began to speak.

"Shut up! Listen! We need to win this and we need a plan about the magic side of things" While James was talking the other two students stopped; they had realised - no plan was in sight. "I'm being serious guys!"

Then Miss Yonda started to head back to the other students. She put her soft hair up in a clip and walked over with her usual smile resting on her face.

~THE SECRETS OF ZELPHA~

"We don't have the strongest magic in the world you know." James finished as the blue carpet reached Miss Yonda's boots. Ellen tried to get information out of James, without telling the whole world about their lack of magic.

"What is so serious about this?" she asked; curiously. All three of the students were cautious of all teachers around them - especially Miss Yonda, the woman right behind them. The trustworthy type but non-magical in this world are sent away - trustworthy or not.

"If we get to this castle we can find the information I need" A scared shaking tone responded. Miss Yonda was increasingly interested in the conversation her students were having; causing Ellen to panic. She quickly changed the topic - drowning in fear.

"Are you really just being a nerd again?" Ellen asked with fear hidden in her voice. Nyx tried to join the conversation; finishing in failure. Miss Yonda, who could sense the tension, started to walk off. Allowing all three students to have some privacy.

"Uhm I really need to know something for a history class" James lied. James was never a liar, he would never lie. *This whole "not magical" thing, must be really dangerous.* Nyx hushed his voice and looked James in the eye.

"Right, what are we going to do about the magic..." he asked as a tsunami of panic flooded the blue team's stand. Just as James was about to respond Ms Gaunt announced,

~THE SECRETS OF ZELPHA~

"James! Here please," she instructed the boy. As he began to walk over to the teacher, Ellen made fun of him for 'being in trouble'. To both of the children's surprise, James turned to them and told them that this was their ticket to ride out of their predicament - as he continued to walk away from the two. Ms Gaunt; quite annoyed, passed him a note. Silent. She was silent. Politely; James requested privacy to read the content inside.

"May I have a bit of privacy to read it?"
Ms Gaunt was not in the mood to be entertaining this behaviour within *HER* world - so she pointed to the moss-infested archway; still silent.

"Thank you" he added before he ran to the moss archway he previously encountered. James opened the envelope, wishing - praying - that the letter inside would help him today. Letter in hand, it read,

James an update. We are still here in the cages. We know your Games are starting soon and I'm sure we are thinking the same thing. Your team needs to be with us. Look, we don't have the time to explain how but in the envelope I have a bit of magic to share with you and your group. It might not last long and if it runs out on you, you're on your own. Take care and best of luck from us
-Aria and the group <3 <3 <3

~THE SECRETS OF ZELPHA~

Ms Gaunt had been pacing up and down her platform waiting for James - to start The Games. Until she finally lost it, she came fuming over, her heavy footsteps became louder as they got closer.

"JAMES! You better hurry up, you ha-" As James finished reading he shoved the envelope into his pocket and spoke over the red-faced teacher that stood ahead of him.

"Thank you so much, mam. You've saved-" Ms Gaunt - who just wanted to get on with The Games - interrupted him.

"Yes yes stop being sappy; enough talking, back to your team stands" Ms Gaunt rushed off from the archway over to her podium - now covered in anger and annoyance. "Silence." as the students continued talking she screamed, "I SAID SILENCE!" causing the whole audience to go silent. "As The Games are about to begin!" she announced as a smile nearly reached her face. All of the remaining students ran to their stands and started chanting, cheering, and clapping with excitement. Mr Gallo stepped forward on the podium, in front of Ms Gaunt - while the students continued cheering over him.

"That's right! All in the audience can we have... GREEN AND ORANGE TEAM PREPARE FOR THE FIRST RACE IMMEDIATELY!" A green and orange beam of light shot up from the sky - causing Ellen to jump into James. James grabbed her wrist and pulled her to the back of their stand - subconsciously causing her to prepare for another scare. Suddenly, a red running track appeared sunk into the ground

~THE SECRETS OF ZELPHA~

sitting snugly; this time making Nyx jump. Magic was most certainly still a fear of the two - even if it was a hidden one. Now Mr Gallo had finished talking, Mr Jaris and Miss Zana led their teams to where Gak stood tall and proud next to the starting point of the race. Bridget wished the orange team luck in The Game and held out her hand for a shake. Hazel grabbed her hand with a smile on her face, until all of a sudden the students heard,

"Looks like someone's gonna need some 'luck magic'" followed up with a giggle from behind her. She instantly let go of Bridget's hand turning around to scold the rude child.

"Shut up Findal! Please ignore him. Good luck guys!" Hazel said, covering up the embarrassing moment. The whole of the green team wished them luck, as they parted ways and Findal mumbled something under his breath. Then, the orange team and green team got into their positions and Yadira began to fly.

" Oh. My. God." Ellen exclaims as she sees Yadira levitating above the other students.

"Look, okay..." James started to stumble upon his words; while concern spread over his face as his eyes tracked Yadira into the twinkling sky above. As James went to continue talking Ellen butted in with a scream.

"How do you expect us to do that?? Do you see them... Yadira - they're literally flying!!" Ellen exclaims; as she starts to be engulfed in a panic attack.

"Keep your voice down. Look, I have a lot of explaining to do and not enough time to do so," James instructed firmly.

~THE SECRETS OF ZELPHA~

"Stop messing around and tell us then!!" Ellen argued. Nyx felt the need to calm Ellen down as she was as bright as the sun. He eventually got Ellen to stop shouting.

"Please let him explain," Nyx - who was often quite jokey - was not having any silly business now. He needed to know how they were going to

"Thank you, Nyx. I'll explain the details later but for now, all you need to know is that I have three crystals. They all have magic in them, however, I don't know what powers they have or how long they will last but it's better than nothing." James shrugs and smiles awkwardly.

"Okay, so you're telling me that I have to learn how to fly by using some random crystal you probably picked from a tree in ten minutes..." Ellen stated with an angry tone. Nyx could finally get some sense out of Ellen and added to the conversation once again.

"Not gonna lie, James, Ellen is making sense for once." He said looking at the two of them wondering what James' plan was, in hopes it was safe - for all three of them. James chuckled, in the hope he was right - not them.

"No, this is the thing - it's magical. You don't have to learn it... you'll go from the ignorance you two have now, to all the knowledge on this power in seconds. You just need to... connect... with the power." he looked at the two, blanketing his fear with a smile. He looked at the two crystals in his hands thinking *this better not hurt my sister. I don't want her to become*

~THE SECRETS OF ZELPHA~

one of them. He finally decided it wasn't his choice - it was hers. He passed the two crystals to the people who trusted him the most - the ones relying on him. Ellen started down at it, recreating the motion her brother did just before.

"I- James are these safe?" she hesitantly asked in fear, with no response. Nyx could tell by the emotion on James's face he didn't know - and didn't want to lie to his sister. To create a sense of security for Ellen, Nyx spoke before James could respond.

"Yeah, like where did you find these?" he asked cautiously.

James went to respond to Nyx but stopped himself before he said a word - instead he responded to Ellen.

"Of course they're safe." Ellen looked at him - coated in fear and doubt. He placed his hand on her shoulder "I promise," this 'promise' sent his mind WILD. *What is wrong with me, I promised I'd never lie to her. Now I'm making promises that I don't know I can keep, giving her dangerous objects. WHAT IS WRONG WITH ME? WHAT IS THIS WORLD DOING TO ME? SOMEONE SAVE ME! PLEASE!* His mind stopped until he suddenly realised *just like my inner child - my overworld self is stuck in this Zelphian mindset. I think this world is changing me for the worse.* James went to reverse his choices - take back what he said until Ellen stopped him by saying.

"You know what we seem to be stuck in this world so who cares" as she put the necklace around her neck. James felt

~THE SECRETS OF ZELPHA~

like a monster. *Am I trapped in a monster?* His sister had trusted him, and he lied. *I LIED. I LIED. WHY DID I LIE?* Nyx saw the lie, he knew that James wasn't aware of what would happen or if they were safe - yet he didn't seem to care. What was he going to lose? He had NOTHING to lose. He placed a scared mask on his face and said

"Oh, my dear goodness okay okay okay." then put his necklace on at the same time as James. Ellen looked around; expecting a scare, a change. Nothing. This necklace did nothing. James zoned out, he had connected with the power - it had been quite some time since he had connected with a crystal. A funny sensation travelled from his head to his toe.

"I- Nothing has happened. James nothing has happened!" Ellen shouted, increasing in fear. James smiled - he may have made a promise he couldn't keep but for now, he could continue to hide it.

"Nothing you say..." he giggled "Nyx come here" In fear that the power had taken over James - Nyx took two small steps toward him. "You ready?" he asked with a comforting smile on his face - causing Nyx to come out with a nod. He counted down from three and suddenly James was gone and Nyx collapsed. Without hesitation, Ellen dropped to the ground and grabbed Nyx. *NO! NYX! WHAT IS IT WITH THIS BLOODY MAGIC!!* Ellen's mind screamed so loudly, that it was as though people could hear it. Suddenly the boy's body she was leaning over, sank. As he sank Ellen tried to grab his hand and pull him

~THE SECRETS OF ZELPHA~

up; no matter what she did, the unconscious boy kept sinking. Until he was gone? To Ellen's surprise, she instantly heard Nyx's voice from where James had stood previously. *WHERE IS JAMES? WHAT ON EARTH IS GOING ON?* All of a sudden; everything Ellen envisioned undid itself, as though it never happened. James and Nyx stood side by side looking at Ellen on the floor.

"Oh my god, it worked!" James shouted in excitement. Nyx on the other hand was not so excited - more dazed.

"I- just I saw myself but it wasn't myself, yet I wasn't myself I was, I was James? Wh-what? Am... am I dreaming? Wake up Nyx" he mumbled, each word on top of another. Suddenly, the realisation of what just happened hit Ellen in the face. Her jaw dropped in pure shock. Magic.

~6~

GAMES BEGIN

Blue team! Blue team! Blue team! The crowd had gone berserk. The constant yelling of 'blue team' destroyed Ellen's train of thought; as she was dragged back into the 'real world' she realised what was going on.

"Oh no no no" she mumbled under her breath, not wanting to gain the attention of the other two. However, this didn't quite go to plan as James had heard her and turned to look her in the eyes.

"Hey, Ellen, it's okay, just stay strong and remember to use your powers," he said with a smile on his face. She sent a smile back and continued mumbling to herself, slowly becoming less worried. Until Mr Gallo interrupted James' reversing of Ellen's state of mind.

"Teachers, please lead your teams to the starting point." He directed. Miss Yonda gave her a comforting smile - unlike the last time she received this smile, she didn't calm down. The nervousness was so overwhelming, that nausea started to form in the very bottom pit of her stomach. She turned to her left to see Mr Lokin lead his students to the starting point of the race - this most certainly didn't help. The red team was very different from the blue team. Mr Lokin led them with a straight back - looking proud of his team until you saw his face. You could see that his green eyes stopped shining many years ago, and were resting above big purple eye bags. His face drooped down - this man most certainly didn't look proud. Behind him was Myrtle, who stood side-by-side with Laryse. Her facial expression sent you the message that she knew she would win. She just knew it. This brought Ellen down until she saw Laryse next to her. The girl looked exhausted - as you would from standing next to Myrtle. Her head drooped down, and for the first time; Ellen felt sorry for her. Behind the two stood Evelyn. The proud girl was happy she made it to the final, a soft smile sat on her face. Exhausted from her hard work - her back wasn't as straight as Mr Lokin's, but she had made it this far, how could she be upset?

"And Ms Gaunt, BEGIN!" Mr Gallo shouted above all the chanting around him. For the final time today, Ms Gaunt pressed a button and the beams at the red and blue teams stands lit up.

"Three... Two... One... GO! Don't forget your powers!" All six of the students sprinted off as fast as they could until Nyx decided it was time to use his powers. The first team to use their

~THE SECRETS OF ZELPHA~

powers was most likely to win, they're the first to take charge of The Game.

"Here I go!" he shouted. All of a sudden Laryse fell to the ground sinking through the track beneath her, as Nyx took her place. He continued running - now looking like and taking control of Laryse.

"Woah, I smell" Nyx whispered under his breath, suddenly he realised he had to start his plan. "Myrtle!" he shouted out loud for all to hear. Myrtle slightly slowed down to turn her head and look at "Laryse", until she realised Nyx was nowhere to be seen.

"Where is that idiot!" she questioned in anger. *Nyx doesn't have magic!* she thought to herself wondering what had happened to her mind or even; her vision. She continued to search the area for Nyx while lightly jogging, now behind many members of the blue team. While Myrtle was looking for him Nyx continued to speed ahead in the body of Laryse. Suddenly she turned to look at Nyx who now turned back into himself, causing Laryse to arise from the ground she had sunken into. Myrtle - now one of the most confused people in this game turned to Laryse and shouted

"Laryse, you little backstabber - don't you want to win?!" She continued to run while looking back at Laryse until a voice appeared in front of her - it was Nyx.

~THE SECRETS OF ZELPHA~

"Of course I do!" he responded. Myrtle was now infuriated by the thought of the blue team having magic. Her face went redder than the jumper under her jacket.

"How the hell are you two so far ahead?" Laryse wailed in exhaustion while trying to catch up to the two of them. Still holding her determination to the red team winning, Myrtle scolded the girl behind her.

"No time for talking Laryse... we can't lose this." James - who had seen this whole thing go down - decided to copy Nyx's idea. *It shouldn't be too hard to fool Laryse... right?* James was most certainly right. He transformed into Myrtle, causing the girl to sink into the ground.

"Time for you to be fooled, shouldn't be too hard with it being YOU" forgetting he had the voice of Myrtle. This was until Laryse reminded him.

"Myrtle, you said no talking" she commented. In the realisation that he contained the power of winning this race, James responded to Laryse.

"Well, I changed my mind... look at how far behind poor Ellen is, let's have a quick rest" A smile grew rapidly on James's face.

"But that's just dumb" Laryse responded, curious as to whether the woman who appeared to be Myrtle ahead of her was serious, actually wanting her to take a break from running. James wanted to put this girl in her place.

~THE SECRETS OF ZELPHA~

"Remember who you are, Laryse, you're the dumb one here, not me," he said with more sass than the real Myrtle herself. No longer questioning her seriousness - Laryse sat down leaning against a tree from near The Games - while James sped off ahead of her.

"I wonder how long I'll be here for," Laryse added to herself. Ellen caught up - now passing Laryse as the real Myrtle rose from the ground, turning James back into himself.

"What are you... WOAH, you really aren't the smart one here falling for what JUST happened, come on!"
It only took a few seconds for Myrtle to realise what had truly happened, and for her to get up and start running, dragging Laryse along with her. Myrtle used a speed boost finishing at the same time as Ellen. Mr Gallo ran over to the children in exhaustion, removing the effects of the potion. He walked over and spoke to the teams ahead of him.

"Good game guys! Seemed really interesting there, never saw that power before, blue team, nice one!" James politely thanked the teacher ahead of him, however, Ellen and Nyx were more interested in the red team sitting on the floor beside them. Myrtle's face was filled with anger - nearly to the point steam blew out of her ears. Ellen continued to examine the team beside her until the yellow and green team rushed over. James was engulfed in a hug from Reid. Everyone went to speak to James while Bridget and Coverly gave their hands to Ellen and Nyx - helping them up from the floor. The two students got up

~THE SECRETS OF ZELPHA~

hugging the girls in front of them. Bridget felt proud of Ellen - holding a big smile on her face when looking down at the girl in her arms. After they let go they rushed over to James, where everyone was congratulating each other for their success in the practice Game. James was over the moon. All of the teams headed to their stands ready for Mr Gallo to announce the winners of the practice trial Games of 2024. Mr Gallo stepped onto the floating platform with Ms Gaunt to his left, she nodded. It was time... time to announce the winners of the trials.

"Okay in 3rd place we have... green team" The crowd went crazy in excitement and hope that they were 2nd, or even that they were good enough to reach the golden 1st place. Mr Gallo continued "In 2nd place we have... red team which leaves our 1st-place winners for this year's practice Games being blue team!" The whole crowd clapped and cheered as the green, red and blue teams walked towards their selected podiums. Ellen began screaming in excitement, jumping around and holding James and Nyx's hands. As the red team rushed to the 2nd place podium Myrtle walked to Mr Gallo shouting in anger and upset.

"What? How? That's not fair!" she shouted at him. Now annoyed at being shouted at, Mr Gallo placed his calm mask over his face. He spoke to the girl calm and controlled - hoping Ms Gaunt wouldn't have to get involved, creating drama.

"I'm sorry Myrtle but the places in that previous Game were: Nyx, James, Evelyn, Ellen, you, and then Laryse." After Myrtle heard Mr Gallo state Laryse came last, she stormed off to

~THE SECRETS OF ZELPHA~

the poor girl before he could even say anything more. Myrtle was furious - so much so that people assumed steam really would start coming out of her ears.

"Laryse you idiot, that's all your fault." Laryse looked down at her feet, slightly shocked, she wasn't disappointed, just scared of Myrtle and hated getting yelled at, especially in front of everyone else who was around.

"Well done guys!" Dusk congratulated them with a huge smile slapped on her face.

"Thanks!" James beamed full of excitement. He had a huge smile plastered on his face. Ellen thought it was going to reach his ears. He loved seeing Myrtle being the wound-up one for a change. While watching Myrtle scream at Laryse, the green and yellow team ran over to Ellen, James and Nyx with happy expressions.

"You really played Laryse there, she looked like a huge idiot," Reid shouted, starting to loosen the grip of the hug. He kept laughing as he had the situation still replaying in his head, over and over again.

"Yeah I'm sure she did," James replied, with a satisfied smile.

"Hey, at least we came second," Evelyn said softly, trying not to stir Myrtle up even more. She was looking down to not draw attention towards herself but sadly she drew Myrtle's glare onto her.

"Shut up nerd." Myrtle spat with gritted teeth.

~THE SECRETS OF ZELPHA~

"Yeah, nerd" echoed Laryse.
Evelyn flinched but looked up at the two who were sharply looking between her and the blue team as they celebrated their win. She sighed before breathing in to get her bearings while looking at the other two girls.

"Hey, I am just being optimistic-" Evelyn tried to say before Myrtle cut her off.

"Can you all shut up? Let's go stand on our little 2nd place podium... you two are so embarrassing." Myrtle huffed before stomping her feet towards where Mr Gallo wanted them to go.
The two girls followed her, Laryse with her head stuck high and mighty - while Evelyn had her head slightly down, trying not to look towards Myrtle or even Dusk. Even Myrtle had a small huff towards the podium, almost bumping into Ellen on the way up the steps. Ellen glanced at Myrtle before skipping a few steps away from the red team. The blue team walked towards the highest podium, while the red team went onto the slightly smaller podium. James looked at the red team and saw that Evelyn was just shuffling her feet while looking towards the ground while Myrtle was clenching her fists before crossing her arms in front of herself.

"Did I already say this is so embarrassing?" She huffed again.
Evelyn looked at Myrtle, and a small frown graced her face. Thinking, Evelyn contemplated speaking as she looked at Laryse

~THE SECRETS OF ZELPHA~

and Myrtle. Laryse was glaring at everyone - especially those in the blue team, while Myrtle was heavily glaring at Ellen and Nyx. Getting confidence, she lifted her arm a bit and opened her mouth to speak.

"No, you said-" Once again, Evenly was cut off.

" Ugh! Who asked for you to speak?" Myrtle glared at Evelyn while Laryse sniggered at her.

Evelyn sighed before looking back down. She knew that when she spoke, Myrtle was going to take her frustration out on her again; but as long as she doesn't have to listen to Myrtle complain anymore, she'd be fine. After a few more words, all the students started walking back towards the school. Myrtle and Laryse started to shove students out of their way before walking briskly towards the school, Evelyn just walked calmly behind them. Ellen hopped down the podium with Nyx and James and they started walking.

" James, how did you do?" Nyx asked him.

" I did good, but I was exhausted at the end." James sighed before looking towards Nyx.

He was slightly panting from the running. Nyx's arms were shaking from the adrenaline of using magic for the first time. James looked around to see the other students hanging about with their teammates. Stretching his arms after feeling the effects of the transformation magic, James saw Nyx clenching his hands and shuffling his legs.

"Yeah, you still need to run even after transformations."

~THE SECRETS OF ZELPHA~

Nyx sighed softly, as his eyes met James.

"I just didn't expect the race to be that long," James stated with a look of exhaustion on his face.

Nyx looked confused at James. He didn't feel like the race was that long, but he didn't question it. James rubbed the back of his neck as he looked at Ellen to see if she was okay. She was slightly shaking but he didn't know if it was from adrenaline or exhaustion. Nyx looked between the two siblings before focusing on James to continue the conversation.

"Maybe the transformations tweak the time?" Nyx questioned

"We have to be prepared for more magic things," James stated.

He had a serious look on his face; however, his apprehensiveness was obvious. Ellen looked at the two before speaking her mind. Her tone showed James that it was a mix of fear and exhaustion. He wanted to comfort her but knew she had to be strong when dealing with the school.

"This magic stuff scares me" Ellen responded she was still feeling weak from the race.

"So that's why you didn't use it, right...?" He questioned. James looked at her and couldn't help but feel a little worried. He pushed it all to the back of his mind however and awaited Ellen's response.

"Yeah, I guess..." She said quietly.

~THE SECRETS OF ZELPHA~

Before he was able to reply, a booming but polite voice interrupted him. All three turned towards Mr Gallo as he approached them.

"BLUE TEAM! Can I speak to you, everyone else please follow Ms Gaunt." Mr Gallo interrupted; Ellen almost appreciated this however she did not want to discuss magic anymore.

"Okay... Nyx, I have something to tell you." Mr Gallo continued speaking.

Nyx was physically jumping up and down excitedly. Ellen sniggered at his behaviour while James facepalmed. They both knew that Nyx was being impatient with what the teacher was going to say, but was also trying to be polite towards him.

"Okay. I'm excited!" Nyx replied enthusiastically.

"You don't even know if it's good or bad yet." Ellen chuckled softly at her friend's ignorance.

Nyx turned sharply towards her, a small pout on his face. He frowned softly at Ellen before grinning. Ellen shook her head at Nyx's facial expression.

"Ellen we have won! Why would we get a bad thing? That wouldn't make any sense. Either way, I wanna know what it is." Nyx was as curious as ever contemplating what the prize could be. He wanted to hear what the teacher said but others kept the teacher from explaining the prize.

"Nyx you are staying at the castle." Mr Gallo revealed towards the three.

~THE SECRETS OF ZELPHA~

James's face went from calm to shock. Ellen looked at the teacher with wide eyes and a slightly open mouth. Nyx looked confused before the words finally settled in his mind. He smirked as he looked at James's shocked face. Nyx knew that James wanted to look at the library - like the nerd he is.

"WHAT!?" James shouted excited about what was ahead he immediately calmed himself down and continued to speak, "Uh..sorry! What! Really?"

"Umm okay then." Nyx didn't seem quite interested in it, but he now had something to rub in James's face. Mr Gallo explained what time he needed to be ready to get to go to the castle tomorrow and then led the team back to the school.

Ellen and Nyx opened their eyes, arms stretched, although they couldn't go outside and there were no windows they felt a beautiful day ahead. James rubbed his face; getting the sleep out of his eyes- putting his book down, he had been awoken by Nyx's snoring. Nyx, bursting with excitement, was the first to talk.

"I'm so excited to explore this castle!" he said a little too loud for James' tired ears to handle. He gave Nyx a look and pulled the blanket back over his head. Ellen, now fully awake, did the favour of handling Nyx this time in the morning.

"Wait... so you can just explore without permission?" Nyx sat perplexed at the question. What would he be allowed to do? Was this just a way of Gaunt keeping him imprisoned? Nyx

~THE SECRETS OF ZELPHA~

took a deep breath and stopped these thoughts from flowing through.

"Well I don't know yet, I need to find out!" All James wanted was to sleep. *But no! James isn't allowed to sleep because these two have been talking for an eternity!* James shouted in his mind - he really didn't like the man he was becoming, he always put family and friends first no matter what. Now he just began to feel selfish. *I just want to leave this place.* He told himself off in his mind and decided it was finally time to get up.

"Ellen, we probably should go eat breakfast, we're gonna be late," He said, in the hope of bringing their conversation to an end. The two hungry students ran to the door, dragging James out of bed and headed up the stairs. As they had only just woken up they looked absolutely dreadful. Hair in disarray, face drooping down with eyebags to the floor. Yet they didn't care - all they did was brush through their hair with their fingers.

"YES! I'm starving!" Ellen responded.

"Okay, let's go." And with that, the siblings walked out of the room. Not wanting to be late they began to speed up, bumping into Mr Gallo in the corridor. He looked down at the children - unable to find a particular emotion or intention in their faces, so proceeded to question their need to be running.

"We're heading to get breakfast," Ellen replied, not even aware of her own emotions. She didn't know whether to be excited for Nyx or worried. This place was full of mysteries and secrets. A story was never fully told at Zelpha, making this

~THE SECRETS OF ZELPHA~

"amazing castle" seem dangerous. Mr Gallo looked the siblings up and down then checked the shiny silver watch that sat snug on his wrist, shimmering so much it nearly blinded Ellen.

"Well then go! You will be late" and with that the two students ran off, heading for the staircase. As the two students ran further and further into the distance, Mr Gallo stood against the wall by the blue team's dorm room. He huffed and checked his watch, then went silent. He was the headteacher the students relied on for a little bit of happiness. He had to be polite here. He let Nyx know he had one minute to gather the rest of his things and be ready to leave the room.

Nyx opened the blue team's door and walked out, bag in hand. As his smile finally formed on his face. He thought he was going to miss his dorm room when in reality he missed the feeling of home and just used this dorm as a temporary placeholder. Realising that blue teams dorm wasn't his home he continued to walk with a straight posture, pushing out his chest next to Mr Gallo, still holding that same smile on his face. They headed to the teacher's side of the school - Nyx now allowed in an out-of-bounds area, on their way to the new adventure ahead.

~7~

CASTLE EXPLORATIONS

They reached the main castle grounds, where Gak was seen writing at his desk. The whole room was made out of some dark blueish-black brick, contrasting against the off-white sanded-down rock roof. Gak's table was a dark wood, oval-shaped counter in the middle of the room. With a candle-lit chandelier hanging above his head. It looked magical, Nyx had been here before but never paid that much attention to all the small details around him. There were six bookshelves, three on each side of the room. They were taller than the young boy himself. They looked magnificent, complementing the room perfectly. Above these bookshelves were two balcony-looking platforms, made of a dark red brick. It looked newer than the rest of the ancient room, left yet to be decorated. Nyx's mind whizzed with ideas of what this room could be filled with, books, seating for reading, or maybe even an area for a book group! In front and behind Gaks desk were two other rooms. This whole

~THE SECRETS OF ZELPHA~

place was extremely open-planned yet still had a full cosy feeling to it.

    Mr Gallo let Nyx be aware that Gak would be looking after him during this time - and the castle's housekeeper may arrive every now and then to check on him. They both headed up the stairs ready to see where Nyx would be spending his nights. Once he reached the end of the never-ending staircase he ran over to a window and looked out of it. He had now realised how high they were from the ground - hundreds of metres high and he realised he wasn't at the tallest part of this beautiful castle. Oh no, this went much much taller and just got more astonishing as you went up. There were five turrets, one at each corner of the castle and one in the centre, the central one was dome-shaped leading to a point at the very top. In that exact same red brick, Nyx had previously seen in the other room. It was beautiful, it was even his favourite colour, as though it was waiting for HIM to arrive. One turret was made of the same blueish-black as the walls of the library. It was so high, Nyx could barely see the top. One of the turrets was destroyed, it seemed to be blown up.

Though it represented something these people didn't like, that scared Nyx until he moved to the other window, where he saw the most extravagant tower ever. It was a tower twenty or so metres above his, holding a massive clock tower at the top, which he had to crane his head out the window to look at. The clocktower was grand and beautiful, he stared at it in awe. It

~THE SECRETS OF ZELPHA~

occurred to Nyx that this is what made everyone aware of the time in Zelpha's school, it had to be due to the sheer size of it. Around the tower was wood, very similar to the wooden desk in the library, yet it was more like bark than planks. It clung onto the clock tower and grew into a cherry blossom tree. It spread out in all directions with pinks and whites, small magical particles swarmed around it - like fireflies hiding within a forest, which seemed to be minuscule - due to how high up it was - flowers grew off it in all the colours you could imagine. It must have been ten or so times bigger than the average tree. He stared at it looming over him, it felt so unreal.

 He turned to Mr Gallo and smiled. He sensed a feeling of home around him. The whole place was calling Nyx, telling him this was where he truly belonged.

 "Gak will take you to take part in any Games and see your friends at 10 am each day, meaning you will most likely be back here for midday." Mr Gallo explained to the student with a beaming face.

 "This is perfect, I mean look at these views! Thank you so much for this amazing opportunity, sir." Nyx said with a smile not leaving his side.

 "You're a good kid, the prize definitely went to the right person," This made Nyx's eyes come close to crying, this was a feeling like never before. He felt warm, within a home environment - and with that, Mr Gallo smiled back at Nyx and left the room. Hearing the footsteps fade away Nyx began to

~THE SECRETS OF ZELPHA~

unpack his things into the pile of barrels to his left. That's when he realised he had not properly looked at his room, he just ran straight out to the window. The room was cross-shaped, with the stairs to get up there tight in the centre. There was a pile of barrels - three to be exact - covered in split ends and a dark brown rope around the rim of the barrel. It had clearly been recently replaced, it looked a lot newer than the wooden barrels themselves. Inside the barrel were a few items of clothing, Nyx put his things into the empty one and turned around to look into the other section of the room. His bed looked much softer than the one in his dorm, it had an oversized cosy-looking grey blanket neatly tucked into the top with the softest-looking pillow ever. The rim of the bed was huge, making it seem more and more extravagant. He wanted to make this place seem like home, yet he had nothing from home, whatever home was. He turned the other way to see a desk which was clean and tidy with a small bamboo plant on top. Then in the final corner, there was a small collection of bookshelves with a lectern similar to what Ms Gaunt read from, however, this one was blank. An unlit lantern sat on top of the shelves, most likely due to the large open windows on all three sides.

"No problem," Mr Gallo called out, "see you soon." Nyx snapped his head over to look at him as he descended the stairs.

"Bye Sir! Right, time to get my stuff away" Nyx muttered to himself as he placed his stuff on the bed.

~THE SECRETS OF ZELPHA~

Silently, he took clothes and other stuff out of the case and into the barrels. Making sure that it was organised to his liking, he glanced around one more time before sighing. Nyx paced around a bit thinking of what he could do at the moment, as he started getting bored.

"Right, let's go have a good time at the library, and see what's there" He snapped his fingers before going down the stairs.

"I wonder why James was so interested..." He muttered to himself.

At a slightly faster pace, Nyx walked down the flight of stairs towards the library. Huffing at the bottom due to the amount, he caught his breath before continuing. Glancing around, Nyx didn't say anything but just pondered. Wondering how old this castle was and was just generally curious. Without realising it, he was already at the entrance to the library. Shaking his head, Nyx looked around and saw Gak - sitting at a table with a book and quill.

"You alright Nyx?" questioned Gak at Nyx's silent stare.

"Uh, yeah thanks" Nyx responded. He tilted his head, questioning Gak. Sadly, Gak didn't seem to figure that out. He just sat there with the book on the desk, flipping to a new page. Nyx's eyes roamed around the room in silence before Gak broke it.

"Welp, I'm going to just be here writing my book... come over if you need any help." Gak looked back down at the pages in

~THE SECRETS OF ZELPHA~

front of him. Nyx walked closer toward Gak to see what he was writing.

"Oh, I didn't know you were writing a book! What's it about?" the question fell from Nyx's lips as he peaked over Gak's shoulder.

Gak slightly covered the page he was currently reading before looking at Nyx. Thinking that Gak was writing something personal, he backed off a bit. Gak's shoulders slumped a bit before perking up as he turned his head toward Nyx.

"Oh, just a group of friends that get brought to the school and must take part in The Games, I might sell it," Gak answered.

He looked very proud of his writing, Nyx smiled at Gak's resolve and goal with his book. While he didn't know Gak's writing style as he didn't want to be rude at looking at the book that Gak was trying to hide on the open page, Nyx knew that Gak's attention to detail was being fully used.

"Sounds good! Welp, Imma have a look around." Nyx walked away from Gak and turned slightly towards the bookshelves.

"Enjoy" was Gak's quiet response - his full attention to writing.

Nyx shook his head at Gak before bringing his eyes toward the section he was now in front of. He was extremely confused at how it was organised, many of the books looked heavily out of place... He saw a book that was titled 'The' near a

~THE SECRETS OF ZELPHA~

book titled 'Bad'. It took a bit for him to realise that the following letter of the 'The' book was 'B', making it organised. Shaking his head at his stupidity, he looked towards the 'D' section. Searching for a few minutes, he didn't see anything that caught his eye. Nyx sighed as he pondered in thought, one book finally did catch his eyes after a couple of minutes of searching.

"Hm... what's this? '*The Jails*' written by... JANE GAUNT?!" He lowered his voice after his shock-filled shout.

"Let's see what this is about... this... is really weird." He stated as the book was flipped to the first page. The page stated that the book was a fiction book, very strange as most books that were fiction don't state it as fiction.

"Why is she so obsessed with making people aware it's fiction... that's just strange" mumbled a sniggering Nyx. He sighed and brought the book toward the nearest table. Sitting down, Nyx just read out loud the book for a while - pausing here and there to readjust his sitting position or to flip the page. Taking a small break, he saw Gak stand up and go to refill his ink bottle for his quill. Stretching and yawning, Nyx looked back down to read; without him knowing - ten minutes had already passed. He jumped as he felt a hand touch his shoulder. Turning his head, Nyx saw that it was Gak trying to get his attention. Sighing to calm his racing heart, he looked at Gak's face. Gak had a small smirk on his face, but that quickly went into a small smile.

~THE SECRETS OF ZELPHA~

"Nyx, can you go to your room? I've got a housekeeper to give you a few outfits to wear to dinner tonight... Can you please be there at 7 pm?" Gak asked him.

Taking his hand off Nyx's shoulder, Gak started walking toward where he left his book and quill so he could put them away.

"Okay sir!" Nyx politely replied while he headed to his room skipping joyfully like there wasn't a thing in his world to worry about. He was too excited about dinner to worry about anything.

"Oh my, these suits are amazing!" Nyx exclaimed excitedly, quickly giving all the options a look. His smile grew bigger and bigger with each suit he looked at. After looking at all the different suits he was offered he ought to try them on.

"Let's try some on." He picked up the first suit and scanned it. He wasn't too sure but tried it on anyway.

"This is nice, it's just too grand for me," Nyx stated, he twirled slightly looking at the suits from all angles then decided to put a different suit on.

"Oh niceee." He told himself, feeling confident in the outfit he put on. He spun lightly to get a good view but was startled as he heard the door open. It was Gak.

"Hope I'm not disturbing anything, oh wow that suit fits you nicely," Gak stated, slowly backing out of the room.

"You think?" Nyx asked, still looking in the mirror not too certain about how it looked. He felt confident but something just didn't feel right.

~THE SECRETS OF ZELPHA~

"Yeah, looks awesome! Have you tried the others yet?" Gak questioned looking at the other suits that were put out to be tried on.

"I tried on that one, too fancy for me though..." Nyx replied, pointing at the first suit he had tried on and holding it up for Gak to see.

"That's okay! Try the other, I'll give you some space." Gak said as he closed the door and made his way out of the room.

"Okay!" Nyx shouted into the corridor. He quickly changed into the last suit so Gak didn't have to stand outside for too long. He had a glance into the mirror and was in awe of what was staring back at him.

"You may come in!" He shouted out to Gak. Signalling for him to come back in and see what he thinks about the last suit.

"Oh my, that's definitely the one, this will be your first impression to Midnight. She is our housekeeper, I'm sure she'll love it!" Gak said as soon as he walked through the door and saw Nyx. He felt proud, something he hadn't felt in a while. It was nice to him that he was proud and still able to feel it.

"I can't wait!" Nyx jumped on the spot with a huge grin plastered on his face and kept checking himself out in the mirror, looking back at Gak a few times.

"Let me take you downstairs, follow me," Gak ordered gently as he left the room with Nyx still in it.

~THE SECRETS OF ZELPHA~

"This is the best, let's go shall we?" Nyx asked but as he turned around he realised Gak had already left and didn't wait for him. After he caught up they walked together in silence until the pair reached the table and took a seat.

~8~

THE DINNER

Nyx entered the dining room, seeing a housekeeper standing beside him. He decided to strike up a conversation with her.

"And what is your name?" he asked, a polite tone lingering in his voice. The housekeeper looked at the boy beside her.

"Hi there! I'm Midnight, and I'm friends with Gak, I guess you could say we're like a small group!" she said holding a soft tone in her voice, she wanted to make Nyx feel welcome. He was in a new world and had now just moved from where he began to settle. *It must be hard for him*, Midnight thought to herself.

"Well, it's lovely to meet you!" Nyx exclaimed, feeling more comfortable than he had ever felt.

"Lovely to meet you too, I should probably go and get your food if you two would like to sit down." Midnight spoke so quickly, she knew she wasn't allowed too much time to chat.

~THE SECRETS OF ZELPHA~

Nyx examined her face before she rushed off to get the food. She was smiling - yet it wasn't a real smile. After his time here, all the secrets, all the lies, Nyx realised what was and what wasn't a true facial expression. Under Midnight's mask of happiness, was a splash of guilt. Almost like she had more privileges than the ones she loved. *That's strange* Nyx thought to himself *she's only a housekeeper... right?*

As Midnight ran off, Nyx switched his attention to the room he had just entered. There was a dark wooden table sitting perfectly in the centre, fitting in with everything else in the room. It rested on a dark grey carpet, illuminated like there was a spotlight shining on it. Around the table were four big chairs, with white shiny plates in front of each one. In the centre of the table was a collection of candles, with two flowers in maroon-clay vases on either side. The rest of the room was shadowed out, there were two exits in the corners, one where Midnight had rushed to. Lanterns were hanging above the entrances, yet the rooms themselves looked dark and mysterious. On either side of the table were two large bookcases filled with books small and big, old and new. This was where all the answers to many questions could be found. In front of the table - right ahead of Nyx was a fireplace, the fire was a strange blue colour *welcome to the world of magic I suppose* Nyx thought to himself. Gak sensed the silence around him and broke it,

"Let's sit shall we" and with that the two sat at the table, Gak at the head, Nyx to his left.

~THE SECRETS OF ZELPHA~

"So how do you like the school?" Nyx didn't think twice, this place was home to him, so he could say what he wanted when he wanted.

"Well not naming names, some of the teachers aren't the greatest." They were both aware of what teacher Nyx was speaking of. "However, other than that, it's pretty awesome!" Gak knew that Gaunt was always watching him, like a laser pointing at its target, burning his flesh. He ignored the comment Nyx made about the teachers, and made the conversation a positive one, not putting Ms Gaunt in a bad light.

"And the adventure has only just begun!" he said with a happy and excited tone, as though he was talking to a seven-year-old, not a seventeen-year-old. Nyx saw the positive intentions behind it and smiled, while Midnight reentered the room with food.

"Here is your starter Nyx, I'll go and get mine and Gak's now" Once again, Midnight did that same rush out of the room that she had previously done before.

"She seems nice," He said as Midnight entered the room with her and Gak's food. She quickly sat down and smiled at the two. Nyx tried to find a way to start a conversation

"Oooo my favourite," he exclaimed, staring down at the meal that sat in front of him. In reality, Nyx had never seen this meal in his life, even as someone with near to no memory, he knew he would remember something that looked like this.

~THE SECRETS OF ZELPHA~

"Anyway, how did you all get to work here?" he asked out of curiosity, he wanted to work here too, or so he thought. Midnight's feeling of guilt slowly subsided and she became more and more comfortable at the table.

All three of them enjoyed their food, and Nyx was completely and utterly full. Their conversation was filled with jokes, laughter, and small talk. Now sitting at his desk in his room, Nyx's mind began to wander, *Home? Not yet, I've only just met these people, for a home to be a home, it needs a family. Family. How could one describe something as complex as a family?* He tried to transition his mind to thinking about something Midnight had earlier mentioned. Ellen and James would get to spend a day at the castle.

James would love it, the history held within the bookcases of this castle was insane. Likewise, Ellen would love the adventure and excitement of a new place with her brother. *Brother. Family. Home.* Nyx's mind had gone back to it, it was like he couldn't escape. This was a good reminder to him that he should go to sleep and so he did. He lifted the blanket and lay on the bed. The blanket was soft, the pillow was just right, and he could hear the life outside his room within the forest - it was illuminated by the dozens of fireflies, yet wasn't too bright, so Nyx could sleep. He was at peace.

Awaken by a bird sitting on the layer of dark brick outside his window. A soft purple bird with a green beak stood proud with magnificence tweeting at him, like an alarm to wake.

~THE SECRETS OF ZELPHA~

He rubbed the sleep from his eyes and looked at the clock by his bed. It wasn't originally there, how did it get there? Nyx saw a note on it signed by Midnight: 'So you're not late for breakfast.'

That was sweet he thought, she must have put it there after the meal last night. The clock made a small ticking sound, so soft that without paying too much attention, you probably wouldn't notice it was there. It read 8 am. He decided to get up and get changed into his uniform, he would be visiting the school soon and didn't want to be wearing a white shirt. That's all he had slept in, an oversized white shirt. Last night was too blurry, all he remembered was peace - that took him away from all feelings beforehand. His floor, however, didn't say peace. His tie rested on his chair, his trousers on one of the barrels (the belt on the barrel beside it) and his blazer over his desk. He got his clothes out of the barrel and began getting dressed. As he finished he put the shirt back in the barrel and suddenly heard a familiar voice.

"I hope I'm not disturbing anything here." It was Midnight, she had both of her hands held behind her back and she was dressed smartly.

"Oh of course not," he smiled at her. "It's a bit early, right?" he glanced back at the clock that read 8:20 am, where on Earth had the time gone? Nyx was now much much more thankful for this clock, as he needed it more than he realised. She smiled, knowing that he had seen the clock.

~THE SECRETS OF ZELPHA~

"Well, I had ten minutes so I thought we could sit together and chat!" she said, holding her usual sweet smile. Nyx waved his hand in the general direction of his chair and stated,

"Oh nice, well please take a seat!" She wandered over to the chair ahead of her and moved his tie to the table. She then looked him up and down. He was wearing a blue hoodie and ripped jeans. Midnight was used to formality. You had to be formal, you had to follow the rules. Midnight was quite shaken by his clothing choice, she asked,

"Is that your uniform?" They would have never allowed her to wear anything like this. Why could he?

"Yeah, my blue team outfit!" he responded with a positive smile.

They continued their conversation until Midnight checked the clock once again. It read 8:28 am. She pointed towards the clock while Nyx's attention was on her and they both got up and began to walk down the stairs.

Eventually, they reached the dinner table and Nyx realised that he was going to visit the school after his meal. It then hit him in the face how much he really needed Ellen and James, so as Nyx and Midnight sat he started eating as quickly as he could. While stuffing his face Midnight let out a little giggle.

"I'm just so excited to see Ellen and James," with a lot of food still in his mouth. Midnight smiled, it was that happy mask with the hint of guild hidden behind.

~THE SECRETS OF ZELPHA~

"Aww, I know the feeling of having a team, or a *group* you could say, they're always there for you." She said wistfully. Nyx wanted to ask what was wrong but also wanted to avoid any awkwardness, so he pushed his plate away and shouted,

"Let's go!" She stopped him. She had to explain that she wasn't allowed in the school, and the only part of the castle's group that could go was Gak. They had to wait. Waiting, it's all we humans do and Nyx hated it. He went to ask why she couldn't go to the castle just as Gak burst into the room.

"Gak!" Nyx shouted as he ran towards him. They waved goodbye to Midnight and left.

~9~

HISTORICAL LESSONS

Nyx ran as fast as his legs would allow him to the two students ahead. They both stood with smiles as he dived into them.

"Ellen! James!" he shouted out loud for the whole school to hear.

"Nyx! We missed you so much!" Ellen responded by hugging the boy back.

"Did you get your timetable?" James asked out of curiosity. Nyx didn't know they got their timetables while he was gone. He checked his pockets in a panic, unaware if he had a timetable until he pulled it out. In the bottom right corner was a little M, he smiled as he opened it up. This girl was able to do anything and everything, *what trained her to be that way?*

"Yes I did, let's compare and see when we have lessons together." With that, the group sat down at the table and checked what lessons they had and when they had them. Their conversation had been going great until the red team wandered

~THE SECRETS OF ZELPHA~

over, crashing into it. Nobody saw them until Myrtle announced,

"You definitely cheated." to Nyx. He sighed and looked up at them, without bothering to lift his head, not giving them much of his attention.

"This is one issue I didn't miss." he announced back, making everyone aware that Myrtle was an 'issue'. Laryse stood behind Myrtle as a form of backup that she definitely didn't want, and Evelyn stood even further back. All of a sudden Bridget walked to the blue team pushing Myrtle as though she didn't even exist.

"Hey, babe! I saw how you did in that competition and wow, you're one extra magic lad huh?" She said, standing confidently behind Ellen's seat and looking directly at Nyx. Nyx went to thank her but Myrtle was not having the way she had just been treated.

"Brie, really?" she butted in. Bridget side-eyed Myrtle, putting her hand on Ellen's shoulder. Bridget paused, she considered if she should even bother talking. She looked back at the blue team and responded with only one word.

"What?" What on Earth could this girl have wanted now? Myrtle walked around the table with Laryse following behind her. She was heading to Nyx.

"I was clearly talking to my best friend Nyx" Myrtle said with all of the sarcasm in the world expressed. Bridget finally

~THE SECRETS OF ZELPHA~

moved her head to look at Myrtle, stopping her from going anywhere closer to Nyx.

"You hear this? I may seem like an idiot but I'm smart enough to know these guys have an IQ in the positive numbers." Myrtle asked what she meant, Laryse being her usual echo. Bridget had already turned back to the blue team, she had already wasted enough time and energy on these idiots, and she didn't want to waste anymore.

"If you let me finish, I'm saying they are smart enough to know not to be your friend." This comment infuriated Myrtle, she nearly went as red as her clothing.

"You used to be cool, man." This made Ellen pause. *How would Myrtle know that? Were they friends, more importantly, WHY were they, friends? What if Myrtle wasn't always bad?* What could have possibly made Myrtle this bad, maybe Ellen was the one in the wrong gang, not Myrtle... Ellen refocused on the conversation and saw the yellow team walk into the room as Myrtle who had not yet spotted them said,

"Waste of time Laryse, come on." She grabbed Laryse's wrist and turned around for Dusk to be in her face.

"Waste of time, that's a bit mean don't you think Myrtle? I thought we were all still friends." As she said it Myrtle huffed and puffed then rushed out of the room as the yellow team joined the blue team and Bridget at the table. The three ask what their original conversation was before Myrtle's usual disruption.

~THE SECRETS OF ZELPHA~

"I was just telling Ellen and James the fact that I get to take them to the castle on one of my days! It's up to them when we do that though," Ellen grabbed Nyx's wrist in excitement and bounced her hands up and down.

"Oh really, who did you meet there?" James asked in excitement. They continued their conversation until the bell rang loudly through the school, giving Nyx a flashback to looking at the clock tower.

"Right, what have you all got now?" He asked as the whole group stood up. They discussed their lessons as they walked to their overgrown magical classrooms.

"Gale and I have a history class with Mr Lokin," James stated as Gale nodded his head in agreement.
Bridget looked over at the paper in Ellen's hand to see what was written down. Suddenly she squealed at what she saw, making the others very concerned. Ellen winced at the volume - since she was right next to Bridget. With Bridget's hand on Ellen's shoulder, she was shaken quite violently by Bridget from her excitement. James looked like he was visibly trying not to laugh at his sister, Ellen just glared at him before trying to pry Bridget's hand off her shoulder.

"Oh my! Rainbow hair girl, do you have Gak now?" Bridget jumped up and down as she said this. Ellen just sheepishly looked at her.

"Yes, yes I do... room 008" Ellen answered, but was kind of cut off by the squealing of Bridget.

~THE SECRETS OF ZELPHA~

"YAY!!! A whole hour with rainbow hair!!" More and more words spewed out of Bridget's mouth that felt like more of a ramble than actual sentences. The others around her just sighed at her while Ellen looked exhausted.

"Oh god." Ellen sighed as everyone chuckled at her. James just patted Ellen on the head while Nyx swatted at her shoulder. The others continued walking towards their classes, making small talk along the way. More and more of them stopped at their designated classrooms, till the group became only Bridget and Ellen. Ellen could still see that Bridget was shaking with excitement but was holding it back as they got closer to the classroom doorway. The two girls looked at each other before entering.

"So rainbow hair, are you excited for this history lesson?" questioned Bridget. Ellen pondered before answering.

"Ehh yeah, my name's Ellen though," Ellen softly glared at Bridget, just annoyed at being called rainbow hair over and over. Bridget just ignored her look and the two finally sat down in their seats.

Gak coughed to gather people's attention as the classroom noise subsided. He looked around the room to make sure everyone was listening.

"The lesson's starting, everyone please be quiet. We're learning about The Games in this school, so please get a book from my desk." After saying that, Gak moved to the side of his desk to reveal a pile of books. Everyone got up and slowly

~THE SECRETS OF ZELPHA~

grabbed a book or two for their partners. Ellen went up and grabbed two books for her and Bridget. Gak waited till everyone was back sitting down before continuing his lecture.

"Originally, there were four main dimensions and this school was built in an empty dimension for the upper-class members of each dimension to do challenges." Gak continued to explain the concept of portals and the beginning of The Games.

After a short while, the words coming out of his mouth turned into mush in Ellen's ears as she looked at the context of the material in the book. Occasionally, she would look up at the board if she heard Gak write something down. The one thing that stood out was the concept of The Games being 'hide and seek' that intrigued her. Gak even explained about a 'Ferryman' and how he was the one who could get people home!

Looking unhappy as usual, Ms Gaunt walked into room 008 and stood at the back of the classroom.

"Hello Gak," she stated bluntly with a blank expression on her face. "You can ignore me. I am just checking in on all the classes." Gak's pale skin got even paler, so he nodded and continued teaching,

"Every year the Ferryman takes the winner back to their dimension. But-" Ms Gaunt, who was now very angry coughed extremely loudly to get the teacher's attention, she directed him out of the room, giving him a death stare. Gak panicked and instructed the students to read pages 23 and 24 of their textbook as it was about the Netheria Dimension; while rushing out of the room. Surprisingly, the students worked. Eventually, Ellen closed her book and looked around at the class, realising they had all done the same. Ellen sat messing with the pen on her table until she made eye contact with Bridget.

"Can you believe all that?" she asked Ellen, looking curiously at the world around her. Ellen sat up from her slumped position and brushed her hair out of her face with her fingers.

"At this point, I think anything is possible here" She stated with a small laugh mixed with a sigh. The bell rang, indicating the end of the lesson, although Gak still wasn't in class, all the students looked at each other, wondering what was best to do next. Bridget, who was ready to leave class, stood up and began to walk out so Ellen followed quickly behind.

The two students continued to talk about their lesson until they bumped into James.

"Hey guys!" James shouted, causing Ellen to jump back. As they both said hello to James he asked what they were up to.

"-Talking about weird portal things and how this world was created!" Bridget shouted. "I just want to know more!" Bridget said. She looked around the room.

"So what was the thing you were learning about?" James questioned, hoping he could tell them more.

"There were portals and stuff that had these holes ripped into them and apparently people got thrown through them but instead of finding a way back they decided to build a school or

~THE SECRETS OF ZELPHA~

something?" Ellen continued talking while walking towards the dorms, the other two followed behind her.

"What happened with Ms Gaunt and Gak? He looked so scared when she left." Bridget questioned, shrugging her shoulders while James looked at the pair, worried and confused.

"I don't know but it's kind of weird how he made us learn about Netheria when she did, instead of The Games. We were learning about that all lesson." Once they had reached the green team's dorm Bridget said bye. Ellen waved bye and continued walking to the blue team's dorm with James.

~10~

CONFRONTATION

"As always this meal is absolutely amazing," Nyx commented. Midnight - who now felt more comfortable being herself around Nyx - began to talk,

"You know you don't have to compliment every meal." She placed her cutlery on the napkin to her left. "Anyway Nyx, I need a word with you, we may stay seated though." Nyx was intrigued, had he done something wrong?

"Yes ma'am?" he questioned. Midnight looked at her hands in her lap, then back up at Nyx.

"Please do not mention me to anyone besides Gak," She requested. Nyx questioned why and got no proper response. There was something about Midnight that wasn't quite right, like she was hiding, or somewhere she shouldn't be. *That would explain why she must not be spoken of, but why would Gak know? Gak does everything Ms Gaunt tells him to.* This sent Nyx's mind racing a little. *Why did Gak follow all these instructions, yet still*

~THE SECRETS OF ZELPHA~

seem to have an okay time with her? What is it with all these secrets? He thought. Nyx came back to the current moment, he then realised he had already mentioned Midnight to Ellen and James, so he truthfully told Midnight. She responded better than Nyx expected.

"I'd like to meet them tomorrow, they seem like nice people and I would also like a word with them about this. For now, let's just eat our food."

Later in the day, Nyx was taken to Zelpha Hall by Gak, while Ms Gaunt was mid-speech. Nyx quickly and quietly sat down, listening to what she had to say. She paused and shot a very disapproving look at Gak.

"Ehem. Today, the green team will be competing against the yellow team. Everyone, please start heading to The Games. Gak check everyone, I'll lead and Mr Gallo follow behind please."

Once each student had been checked and made their way to The Games Ellen, James and Nyx stood at their stands and began to talk.

"Thank god it's not us. I really need to get used to this power" Ellen whispered looking up at her brother. James coughed loudly, searching for something to change the topic to. Ellen took the hint and moved on.

"You realise it's our friends competing..." Nyx butted in breaking the awkwardness.

~THE SECRETS OF ZELPHA~

"Either way just act happy when one wins. They will understand." James responded. Ellen looked up at James and questioned how he was always so positive, always able to find the good in a bad situation.

"Someone has to keep the spirits high in this group!" he responded, as the green team and the yellow team headed to the start of The Games.

"You're good at that you know," Ellen said smiling. After all the pair had been through he was still positive, without James, Ellen couldn't even begin to comprehend how she would have kept going. The pair were so lost in conversation that when Nyx tapped them on the shoulder they realised the game had already started. Ellen and James began cheering for both teams.

Team names were chanted throughout the crowd, as Laryse slumped to the ground in the red team stand nearby, with a slight thud. Her facial expression changed to someone who seemed quite bored.

"Well, I hope they both lose," she pouted. Myrtle moved to face Laryse.

"Laryse that's not possible" she bluntly stated exasperatedly.
Evelyn looked down at Laryse who was still slumped on the ground, then looked up at Myrtle, who sent a shiver down her spine.

~THE SECRETS OF ZELPHA~

"I'm surprised I'm saying this but Myrtle is right," Evelyn added, shaking all over. Myrtle's glare turned Evelyn's ash brown hair to ashes, as she responded with,

"Of course, I'm right you nerd." Suddenly, an expression scarier than Myrtle's appeared on Laryse's face, a sly smile rested naturally on her face.

"Anything is possible with a little bit of magic, right?" Laryse's grin continued to grow bigger and bigger. As to nobody's surprise, Myrtle was concerned at what Laryse had in mind, asking where she was taking this.

Day and night, Evelyn's mind was always thinking of finally being free. Free from HER. She wanted to talk, even if she had one fake friend, it must be better than having no friends; right? Wrong. No matter what Evelyn did, she couldn't escape her power, let alone be her friend.

"Are you going to shut your mouth?" Myrtle rhetorically asked Evelyn.

"Yeah shut your mouth," Laryse repeated. Myrtle instantly moved over to Laryse.

"And, are you going to tell us your plan or not?" She questioned. In response, Laryse looked back at Myrtle holding an anxious expression on her face.

"The idiot is too stupid to make a plan so she wants you to make one for her." Evelyn butted in as Laryse had pointed out that there was an issue but didn't give any details.

~THE SECRETS OF ZELPHA~

"It's too late to make a plan now anyway," Myrtle grumbled, now annoyed at Laryse's idiocy. Ellen strolled into the scene - with confidence.

"It's too late to make a plan anytime unless you want to be removed from The Games,"

Crap Evelyn thought, petrified of how Myrtle would take this conversation.

Without hesitation, Myrtle shoved Ellen into a corner; holding her back. Myrtle's eyes - which were holding complete eye contact with Ellen - their plain red look had now turned fiery-red. This look had a murderous look within them. Her eyebrows furrowed downward, sitting on her fiery red-tinted skin. Her sarcastic smile fell into a dead expression, and Ellen was petrified with fear.

On the other hand, Ellen struggled to break free from Myrtle's grasp. Fear had drained the colour from her already pale skin, and she found it difficult to catch her breath, let alone speak. Though she attempted to shake her head to signal for help and squirmed to break free from Myrtle's hold, she remained trapped. Myrtle began to speak.

"Listen here you little kid, I know your magic is fake… it's got to be, and if you tell a teacher I'll have you sent to the jails with a painful death following shortly after."

All of the commotion had caught James' attention, once he saw what happened he sprinted as fast as he could to his sister.

~THE SECRETS OF ZELPHA~

Finally reaching the scene James jumped onto Myrtle causing her to lose her grip on Ellen; while shouting,

"HEY! Get away from her" James instantly stood up and grabbed his sister's hand, pulling her from the ground. The infuriated voice had now gone calm and soft.

"Hey, are you okay? Did she hurt you?" Ellen looked James in the eye. *The jails* she thought.

"Let's go," James instructed without letting go of Ellen's hand.
Ellen left looking stunned while James dragged her along with a tight grip.

The teams discussed how they both enjoyed their game and how well everyone did. Then Mr Gallo called them both over to announce the winner. All of this took place whilst James spoke to Ellen, trying to sound calm and comforting, needing to find out information on the ongoing situation.

"Hey, Ellen, what did you say over there?" Her initial response was a look, a look to the floor, then back up at him.

"That night you were up late you mentioned the jails, Myrtle said I am going there because I have no magic..." Ellen said - her eyes tearing up.

"You're going to be safe, I'm here. I still have no memory of that night you keep mentioning." Ellen gained the confidence to discuss the night, it felt like she was reliving it but after her situation with Myrtle, it was much scarier and much more real to her.

~THE SECRETS OF ZELPHA~

"You were in the library and you were shouting but you were also this girl and..." Ellen couldn't bring herself to talk much longer, all the flashbacks came flooding through. As Nyx entered the conversation, James looked down and whispered something under his breath. Ellen couldn't make out what he said however it sounded like a name. He looked down, as though something had hit him in the face. Nyx could sense the upset within the conversation.

"What are you guys talking about...?" This caused James to look directly up at the boy ahead of him and talk very suddenly and very quickly.

"Tomorrow I want to go to the castle." As soon as James announced that Nyx knew he was serious so he went straight to Gak explaining that he wanted Ellen and James to go to the castle tomorrow. Gak mentioned that Midnight would not be with them tomorrow, which seemed unusual as she had attended every day Nyx had been there. Yet he ignored it, there was much investigating he had to go into regarding Midnight before asking any questions.

"Right let's get you to the castle, Mr Gallo will get James and Ellen in the morning," Gak replied and with that Nyx and Gak left Midnight sat at the table alone.

~11~

DISCOVERY

Ellen, who had awoken as a ball of energy ran to James' bed and began shouting and shaking the poor boy.

"James! wake up!" she screamed. James suddenly woke up with so much anger, how dare someone wake this man from his slumber? The pretty princess required some beauty sleep. He tried not to scream at the girl standing ahead of him, he didn't want to burst her bubble.

"Give me one good reason why you did that." he looked at her, barely keeping his eyes open. Ellen stopped bouncing as he spoke but when she replied, it set her off once again.

"It's castle day!" There were so many new adventures and experiences lying ahead of the siblings - all James wanted was to lie back down, whereas Ellen was bursting with energy.

"Ellen, do you ever stop shouting?" he asked, drained from trying to drag himself off the bed. Ellen decided to ignore him and get him up quicker. She grabbed his arm.

~THE SECRETS OF ZELPHA~

"Come on James, we have to go!" Ellen said. She was excited to go to the castle, so she rushed James so they could get there as soon as possible

"Alright, fine. I'm up already. Let's go." James answered Ellen with a sleepy face. He had just woken up and he wasn't quite ready to get out of bed yet but he knew he had to go. He got ready to leave the room and faced Ellen, who was already looking at him.

"James, I think that we should say bye before leaving," Ellen spoke before the both of them heard a knock on the door. Ellen walked forward to open the door but was stopped by James.

"I'll answer it." James walked over and opened it. It was Bridget and Yadira who stood there, waiting for someone to open the door.

"Oh wow, guys! I heard the news, you're like royalty now!!" Bridget exclaimed with a face full of excitement and happiness. She was truly happy for her friends, and her tone made that very clear.

"Bridget, just because we are going to a castle doesn't mean we are royalty... sadly," James said while looking at Bridget with a calm and collected face. His expression wasn't a very excited one as he had just woken up.

"Well, I've tried to tell her." Yadira sighs, looking at the floor. She had talked to Bridget about this topic previously as they walked to the blue team's dorm but it was very clear that her efforts were in vain.

"Let's sit down guys!" Ellen said. She looked around for a place to sit. There weren't many options around there, so she pointed at the stone floor.

"Not on that. I think that we should go to our room." Bridget said, looking at Ellen. A rock isn't the best place to sit, so Bridget suggested that they go to the green team's room.

"That's a good idea," James said, shrugging. They started to walk to the green team's room and chatted as they walked. the green team's room wasn't too far so they got there in no time.

"Woah, it's nice in here..." Ellen said, shocked at how nice the green team's room was. The beautiful decorations and things that they did not have back in their room. This room was truly aesthetically pleasing to look at and it made everyone stunned.

"Heya guys," James said, waving at Coverly and Gale. The two had already been hanging out in the green team dorm. They all sat and started chatting amongst themselves.

"Hey," Gale said, welcoming the people inside the room. They sat down next to their friends.

"So, James and I are going to the castle today!" Ellen said excitedly. Her expression was one of sheer happiness and excitement as she couldn't wait to go.

"No way, really?" said Coverly, lifting her head from the book. She was truly happy for her friends since this was kind of a great achievement in her eyes.

~THE SECRETS OF ZELPHA~

"Yeah! They're like royalty now!!" Bridget exclaimed loudly. They were all excited and happy that Ellen and James got to experience such an amazing day.

"You may not be royalty, but you may be famous!" Yadira said excitedly. James looked at her, clearly confused about what she was saying.

"What? Famous?" James asked, not sure how to feel about what Yadira had just said.

"That castle is massive! You could find a window or something that shows the village, we could find out the truth." Yadira said, giving them a suggestion of what they could do to get closer to finding the answers they needed. Ellen and James wanted to find a way to take a look at the village close to the castle.

"Oh my! I never thought of that!" James exclaimed.

"But... how can we prove what we find though?" Ellen asks, curiously. All the students looked at each other until there was a knock at the door, which was opened by Mr Gallo.

"There you are," he sighed. "I thought you would be in your room! Right, are you ready?" he asked the two blue team members who were sitting in the corner of the room.

"I think so," Ellen said while getting herself up. "You ready James?" she asked putting her hand out for James to get himself up with. James had been staring at his shoes for the past few moments thinking.

~THE SECRETS OF ZELPHA~

"A book!" James exclaimed, this he thought would be a way to reveal the secrets of zelpha. That was when he shook his head and realised what was happening. "Uh yeah, I'm ready!" He grabbed Ellen's hand and stood up. James then looked at Yadira and whispered,

"Yadira, a book" she responded with a small smile and a slight nod of her head. James, now knowing that he had a plan, turned to leave the room with Ellen following.

Ellen, James and Mr Gallo left the room, leaving the two teams behind. During this time Mr Gallo gave them some info in between their small talk.

"Some information; breakfast will begin at your arrival, dinner starts at 8 pm and I'll be there at 10 pm to collect you." The siblings acknowledged his statement and continued talking, mindlessly following Mr Gallo until they finally reached the castle.

"So, this is the library and this is where I will leave you, feel free to explore. Gaks there if you need him." Mr Gallo caught Gak's attention and the young man waved as he started to walk over. It was like, no matter where you go, which corners you turn or who you are with, Gak was there - always. Once he reached the group of three, Mr Gallo left to go back to the school. Curious, the children asked what Gak was doing.

"Oh just writing my book, I left some clothes for you in Nyx's room. He's probably there too, all the way up those stairs." His book spiked Ellen's interest. She went to talk about it but realised breakfast would be starting soon and they had to be ready. Ellen looked in the direction Gak was pointing, then up at James.

"I'll race you there!" she said with a grin on her face. With that, she ran off.

"Good luck." Gak laughed and sighed, simply exhausted from the thought of poor James chasing Ellen up the stairs.

Ellen burst into Nyx's room. Nyx dropped the book that he had in his hands onto the bed that he sat on.

"Agh! Ellen!" he shouted. Nobody had this amount of energy here and he had gotten used to it that way. Everyone usually entered calmly and gave him time to realise they were coming up the stairs before entering. Unlike Nyx, Ellen found this hilarious and started giggling.

"Did I scare you?" she asked jokingly, fully aware of what the true answer was.

"Hm, what? Oh no- no not at all." Nyx lied. James entered the room tired and out of breath, shoving Ellen out of the way to make it to the chair that was in the corner of the room. The pair laughed at him as he was tired and in pain.

"Where do you get all of your energy from Ellen?" James questioned as he made it to the chair, flopping onto it.

"You sound like mum…" Ellen mumbled to herself under her breath as her smile faded, she didn't want her mother to be a topic of conversation with him. It wasn't time, not yet. She plastered her usual smile back onto her face as James whined.

~THE SECRETS OF ZELPHA~

"It's true! There were so many stairs," complained James. The two smiled at him and Nyx explained the plan for the day, starting with breakfast.

"Pick an outfit from this pile for breakfast." Nyx sat on his bed and shoved his nose back into his book to allow the students to change in privacy. Ellen chose a loose white shirt and James chose a tighter black one, The three complimented each other's outfits and they began to head downstairs for breakfast.

They entered the room where they would be having their first meal of the day, it was right by the library. In the corner of the room was the fish tank that had previously caught Ellen's attention. Nyx recognised the room they were entering from his meals yesterday.

"Where is Midni-?" Nyx began until Gak cut him off and answered nervously.

"OH! Uhm, she's not here today." Sensing Gak's discomfort, James brought light to the situation. Although, he was very curious as to why Gak cut him off.

"So we have to put up with you all day? Great! Thanks." he joked.

"Put up with me? I think you'd find we are all putting up with you, mister." Gak joked back, which got some laughs and a positive atmosphere. Gak told the group to take a seat while he went to get the food.

The three students sat down and had some small talk about the food they would be getting. Nyx explained that unlike

~THE SECRETS OF ZELPHA~

the school food - which was all from planet Xalnoth - this food was from any planet.

"How'd you know that?" James asked as Gak reentered the room with plates of food.

"Gak told me," Nyx responded. Gak quickly picked up on the conversation the students had been having.

"I told you what?" Gak asked quickly.

"About the school's food..." Nyx responded, curious as to why Gak was suddenly so on edge.

"Well, here's your food guys. It's from Planet Iphus and guess what we are having for drinks!" he said very excitedly. James instantly knew what was coming,

"Prepare-" James stated as Gak grabbed the drinks and rushed back to the table with a shout.

"Fizzle juice!" Gak rushed around passing out drinks buzzing with excitement as James sighed.

After the meal, Ellen slouched in her chair and thanked Gak for the food. He was happily collecting the plates, cups and cutlery when he realised James had not drunk his fizzle juice.

"A bubbling purple froth, yeah... I'm good thanks." James stated, not too happy that he hadn't had a drink. They continued talking about what their plan for the rest of the day was when James got up from his chair and urgently excused himself to go back to the library.

~THE SECRETS OF ZELPHA~

It was now that Gak brought up his book once again, and Ellen's interest spiked back up. *Now my time to ask some questions* she thought to herself.

"Wow, you're writing a book, that's so cool! I'd love to publish a book one day," she explained admiringly. She always found herself writing little bits and pieces, and the last good memory of her mother was reading books. She was sure of the fact that James would love it too.

"You should go to the library and read it," Gak said, surprised that the young girl had taken an interest in what he had seen to be a nerdy hobby.

It was at that time that Nyx headed back to his room and Ellen and Gak went to the library to look at his book. When Ellen made it down to the library she saw James rushing about looking through the bookshelves and flicking through pages, he was having a serious panic attack.

"Woah James, calm down, What on Earth are you looking for?" Ellen asked. James didn't pay any attention to Ellen and continued frantically searching. A moment later, Gak called out for Ellen. She walked away from James, leaving him to his search.

"Ellen! Come on!" She made her way over to Gak and took the book - which was currently written in a blue notebook - that he handed to her.

~THE SECRETS OF ZELPHA~

"So here is what I have so far, what do you think?" Gak asked, excited to have someone else's opinion. Ellen flicked open the book a few pages in and read.

Thud.
Pain ricocheted throughout the girl's body as she hit the ground. The force of the fall had winded her; she couldn't even cry out in pain, audibly at least. All she could do was lie there as she tried to steady her breath. After a couple of seconds, she slowly sat up and clutched her ribcage in agony. With uneven breathing and blurry vision, she looked up slowly to see where she had fallen from, only to find that she was looking up into an infinite void. Surely, she should have died from that height, but why hadn't she? Instead, it had just left her with a bruised back (no broken bones).

As soon as her eyes adjusted fully, her heart started racing as she sat up. Her eyes searched every corner of the small room she was trapped in - she saw nothing, it was all just darkness.

"W-what happened? Where am I?" She gasped, almost to herself. Suddenly, a blinding light burst into the room, spilling brightness everywhere and coating the walls around her. She quickly shielded her eyes before opening them slowly. A large, metal gate was down in front of her, and she could hear voices - *people*.

~THE SECRETS OF ZELPHA~

Suddenly, an unfamiliar voice started to approach her; it sounded urgent.

"Excuse me, child! Yes, you!"

The heavy footsteps became louder as they got closer. The girl could feel her heartbeat pulsing in her ear while her mouth became dry. She looked up to see an older woman, walking quickly toward her.

"That's really good!" the girl said to Gak. "I will have to buy one when I'm home" Gak looked at her, this was the girl that he had found messing about in an out-of-bounds area, and she was now reading and complimenting one of the most important things in his life.

"You're a good kid, after that night I was worried you were another naughty kid I'd have to put up with." Gak smiled, looking down at her.

"No, she really locked me up in there," Ellen responded - referring to when Myrtle had locked her in the control room. Gak continued to look at Ellen, knowing that he should deal with whatever happened to her that night. He knew it had to be him to do it, nobody else.

"Who?" he asked her. Ellen looked at Gak and she went to speak although she cut herself off when she saw James run past from one side of the library to the other, so quick they barely saw him. This caught Gak's attention too.

~THE SECRETS OF ZELPHA~

"He's not okay..." Gak stated jokingly, while also slightly serious. They both had a half laugh until Ellen realised that James didn't drink anything at breakfast, so she left to get him a drink. As Ellen ran out of the room Gak strolled over to James with his hands in his pockets. He leaned against a bookshelf and ran his fingers through his dark red hair.

"What are you looking for? Maybe I can help." Gak offered with a reassuring smile on his face. James went to ask for help but stopped himself.

"I- no. I'll find it myself. Thank you." Could he trust Gak with this information he was trying to find? It seemed like something he shouldn't know about, or even look for. Nobody else had mentioned this before, was it known by all magicals that it shouldn't be spoken about? Will it ruin his cover?

"It's alright, I spend all day writing, it'll be a nice break." Gak pleaded, curious as to what James was so worried about. James looked at Gak. They had created such a close bond over the past year or so, would Gak destroy James' good reputation? Surely he would help him, *Gak doesn't like Ms Gaunt anyway, so maybe he wouldn't tell her?* He decided to take the risk and ask,

"Wh-Whose 'Aria'?"

"James! You didn't drink earlier so I got you water." Ellen shouted from the doorway. Gak's pale face zoned out entirely. James thanked Ellen for the water and took a sip from it. "Take a moment to sit down and relax, you seem stressed," Ellen said to him, pointing to the chair that was placed between the two bookshelves. James, who just wanted to keep looking, told Ellen that he was okay and didn't need to rest; yet this girl kept insisting.

As James took a seat Nyx entered the room, now in his normal clothes. Nyx sat down next to James and started some small talk about what it was James had been looking for all this time.

After a few moments of Ellen and Nyx questioning what was going on, James lost his patience.

"Can we just leave it?!" he asked with a raised tone. Gak shook his head and realised what was going on, he used his authority to help James out. Gak didn't want James telling everyone about Aria, or even thinking about her. This was his issue and somehow the young boy had got himself involved.

"Guys, just leave him be, he doesn't want to talk about whatever it is." He said sternly, the two students looked at their feet as a way of saying sorry. James began to mumble under his breath.

"At least someone understands..." Turning to Ellen he asked. "Anyway Ellen, about what Yadira said, did you see, you know, the thing..." Ellen took a second to realise that James was referring to the village but didn't want Gak to know what they were looking for as he was a teacher.

"Oh no I didn't, Nyx let's go have a look," Ellen responded looking at the two students and grabbing Nyx's hand, ready to leave.

~THE SECRETS OF ZELPHA~

As the two left, James stood up and walked over to Gak's desk and sat with him on the countertop. Gak took a moment to think of how to word all of this to James, this was a topic close to his heart that he wasn't prepared to talk about.

"Look, I don't know how you found out about her but please just stay out of it. You're a smart kid, you'll come across it as time goes on. It'll make sense one day, I promise. For now - don't think about her, just have fun." Gak said in a caring supportive manner, holding in all of his emotions. He hoped it was all a dream and he would wake up soon enough. James looked down at his feet, which were just touching the floor and began to talk.

"It's just, that she has sent me a few letters from her and "the group" to help me and I want to know about her, I know she knows you," James explained to Gak this caused him to instantly look up from the floor to James's face.

"Wait, you've spoken to her..." Gak said, trailing off in his thoughts whilst talking, *who is this 'Aria girl' and why has it impacted Gak so much?* James questioned in his mind.

"She's just helped me by sending me letters, I've never sent a letter back, if I'm honest I don't even know how. I don't know how she gets them to me either. She's not said anything about who she is, just help in The Games and stuff." James stated, feeling kind of down. A negative energy lingered in the air and he didn't know why, but it seemed to be coming from Gak.

~THE SECRETS OF ZELPHA~

"She's still alive? No... it can't be." Gak muttered under his breath to himself, hoping James wouldn't hear. As Gak went to talk to James, Ellen ran into the room while shouting,
"James! Quickly, come here." As she said this she grabbed James by the wrist, dragging him off the wooden countertop and into the turret that Ellen had taken Nyx only moments before.
James' voice turned stern. He was about to find out what he had been wondering all this time, yet Ellen just took him away. Took him away from the answers to all of the secrets in his life. All the secrets he thought were hidden. This was the first time James had ever had genuine anger towards Ellen.
"Ellen! You can't just do that. I was having a conversation, what could be so impo-" James pauses, taking a moment to look out at the area he had been taken to.
"It's the village," Nyx stated, staring straight ahead. James stood looking ahead amazed, they had spoken about this place day in and day out but he never realised they had been right all this time. It felt magical to know they had been right. He stood ahead, looking at this beautiful village that had been so close to them this whole time, an escape from the day-to-day routine, new life, new people, and a new story lay ahead of them. James was so shaken by its reality he didn't know what to say, it was sitting right in front of his eyes.
"I wonder what's living there. Maybe it's dragons and unicorns!" Ellen exclaimed. The group faded out of their trance

~THE SECRETS OF ZELPHA~

with some small talk about this new magical land lying ahead of them, until Ellen grabbed James' hand and began to run off; excited to explore she tried to run. James anchored her to the spot.

"Woah! Calm down, you're not going anywhere just yet. We aren't allowed." he instructed the young girl - bursting her bubble.

"And I'm pretty sure I don't see any dragons or unicorns over there," Nyx told her with a small laugh to himself.

"Ugh! You guys are no fun!" Ellen whined as her mood plummeted to the ground. James instantly knew what to do in a situation like this, giving her a choice.

"No fun, ey? Well go down there and get yourself in trouble then!" She stood unsure of what to do, when it came to decisions, no matter how big or small, she relied on her brother. Meaning she did very little when living without him; she was dependent on him and he would have it no other way. She spent a moment to consider her options and mumbled to herself under her breath before deciding it was best to not go and check it out - at least until they have a proper plan in place.

"So, James, you said you were going to write a book about this. When are you gonna start?" she asked knowing she wanted to join in. His face dropped a little, seeming less himself. Now quieter he mumbled,

"I need to find the book in the library first." He seemed slightly stern towards himself. It was almost as though he would punish himself for not finding whatever he was looking for. This caused Ellen to desperately want to help, but she didn't want to appear too desperate so she calmly asked,

"What's that even about James?" James looked down and kicked his feet, realising it was finally time for him to explain what had been going on to his fellow teammates.

"Right, I can't tell you much about it... but ugh. Right Ellen," James was struggling with how to explain what had happened to Nyx so he looked to Ellen, knowing exactly what to refer to. "You know 'that girl' you saw 'that night' in the library?" James asked her.

"Yeah? Honestly, I thought that was some 'magic' prank." Ellen responded curious as to what this night had to do with a book.

"Well, I want to find out about her. She's spoken to me a few times... but that night was most certainly not me." James said, looking at and kicking his feet once again. He felt as though he had been defeated, now three other people knew about what he was looking for, and he admitted he needed help.

"Woah! Do you know anything about her? Maybe we can help?" Ellen asked rather excitedly. If they found the girl Ellen could ask what she was talking about that night, why she shouldn't trust anyone, and why the girl went to Ellen and not somebody else. She just had so many questions on her mind she could barely think.

~THE SECRETS OF ZELPHA~

This was when Nyx joined the conversation, although he wasn't present that night he was still most certainly interested.

"Yeah, you said you had spoken to her a few times, what did she say?" he asked eager to find out more.

"She has 'a group' but honestly I think I should work on this alone," James stated finally looking back up at the two, he appreciated their help but knew that he didn't have much time to find all of the answers he was looking for.

The word 'group' had caught Nyx's attention, he had heard this word used many times before but he just couldn't think where. As a young boy who has been struggling to remember his life before Zelpha, he sat and thought hard. Where had he heard this word? Seeing Nyx's puzzled face James started to speak to him.

"Nyx'll know nothing, this place holds the information I need to know." As James spoke realisation hit Nyx right in the face and he began to stare into space thinking about how this could relate to some mysterious girl.

"James, that night. You- she... whoever that was, made me read a book. Maybe that's a hint." Ellen started getting annoyed at herself for not being able to identify who this person was. James's tone became the bluntest Ellen had ever heard it.

"What was the book about?" he asked seriously. Ellen took a moment to think, James was serious and she needed to check with herself that she was right before she began to talk.

~THE SECRETS OF ZELPHA~

"Something to do with the Jails, the Deathstar Jails? Maybe..." Ellen questioned herself before she recalled the name. "No! The Deathstone Jails. Myrtle mentioned a jail of some sort and said I am going there because of my lack of magic..." Ellen paused, feeling worried from thinking back to that very moment. "Maybe that'll help?" she ended with. James had that serious expression upon his face once more and bluntly responded.

"Do you have the book?" Ellen looked down, disappointed in herself for not being able to help James.

"No. You... she, dropped it" Ellen explained while still getting confused as to who this soft mysterious girl was. She continued to explain, "She gave me a page of the book but the words had faded when I went to show Gak" Still in his serious blunt tone James asked to see the page, which had now mysteriously had words on it; the same words that had been on it only a few nights ago. Ellen looked confused as Nyx refocused his attention back to the ongoing situation.

"James, do you know the names of "the group" the girl spoke of?" Nyx asked, looking back at him. As James stated that he doesn't know any of the group's names, Nyx explained that he may have an idea of who this group may be. Surprisingly, he didn't want to share this information as he wanted to know more before making assumptions.

"I'll find out, don't worry," James concluded. "Anyway, writing the book, yeah. I'll do it soon, you guys have put me at

~186~

ease, finally knowing I'm not alone." Nyx giggled to himself before jokingly stating,

"Not with Ellen, it's like she's your shadow!" The group began to laugh, as Nyx's sarcastic comment was true.

"What can I say? I just keep him company when he's not with his 'loads of friends'." Ellen replied, hoping to keep up this funny jokey atmosphere.

"Ha-ha, very funny. You guys wanna help write this book?" James asked, hoping for a little help from his friends. They all agreed and went to get to work.

~12~

THE REVEAL

Ellen James and Nyx were now sitting at a table which was upstairs from the library, in a large comfortable-looking room. Natural light flooded in as several archway exits led to balconies, allowing you to see the luscious forest and village that lay ahead. Covering each wall were several bookshelves and many vines hanging from the walls and ceilings. Ellen, James and Nyx sat at a large, grey table in the centre of the room.

Scattered all along the table were journals, books and a large collection of pens and quills. The three were currently jotting down ideas and information they had collected over their time at Zelpha that could connect the dots of the origin of the village. James handed Ellen something he had written for her opinion. Ellen smiled and nodded in approval.

"I really like this James! You're good at writing," she stated as she gently handed the book back over to him. Nyx

~THE SECRETS OF ZELPHA~

looked up from the book he had been staring at, questioning what to write on it for hours and responded to Ellen.

"What did you expect? He's always reading, he must be good at writing." Nyx giggled. James, who was thankful for the compliment, explained his history within the writing world.

"Yeah, I used to keep a diary back home and would write little stories when I first got here, it was pretty lonely you know." This perked Ellen's interest, she had been so hung up on what her world was like without him, that she didn't even consider what his world was like without her. She had always assumed that James had Coverly, Dusk and Gale, so she questioned him. Hoping to get him to finally talk about his feelings.

"Well, I had convinced myself I was going back to you and mum soon so I didn't make any attachments until I realised there was no going home, and I should try and make some friends." James looked down at his feet under the table, he didn't like to talk about his feelings so he didn't come across to others as weak and pathetic, when in reality he needed the release. Ellen's mood had dropped as it had been a while since someone had mentioned her mother, as though she was still alive, she needed more time to get used to it. However, she put that to one side, hoping and dreaming he would move on. Not all dreams come true though.

James thought about his mother and realised he and Ellen had barely had the time to discuss her, how she was doing and what life would be like when they got back to their planet.

~THE SECRETS OF ZELPHA~

Suddenly, James' mind flooded with questions to ask her. He started with the most important one.

"How is mum anyway?" He asked. Ellen mumbled under her breath in response, James assumed she'd responded but couldn't hear so he asked another one. "So yeah, does mum miss me?" Ellen knew that she couldn't lie to her brother, not after all he had done for her.

"Y-yeah! The last time I talked with mum she was really missing you." An awkward silence followed Ellen's words as she got even closer to ripping off her mask of a smile and bursting into tears. Before any tears, rubbing her eyes, she managed to get the conversation going again. "Right, so anyway - how's the writing going?"

James went to respond but was cut off by Nyx. He had been listening to the conversation between James and Ellen and realised she needed a moment outside, so he asked the group,

"Wait, should we look a bit deeper into things right now?" The siblings turned to Nyx and James responded instantly with a naive smile.

"I actually do think that is a good idea, hey Ellen why don't I keep writing while you guys go look? I want to keep writing, I've hit a groove." Ellen jumped out of her seat and began to drag Nyx out of the room. She had to leave James for a moment, a moment to sort out her thoughts.

She turned away from James and grabbed Nyx's wrist. Before he had a chance to get up out of his seat, she'd already started to walk out of the room still holding onto his wrist with a tight grip.

"Ellen... ELLEN HOLD ON!" as though she was deaf she continued to walk out of the room with Nyx's wrist in her hand. Once they had got out of the room Nyx removed his wrist from her impeccable tight grip and looked her in the eye, trying to find out what had happened.

"Why did you rush away from James there? Like, ever since he asked about your mum the atmosphere in the room was rather awkward." Ellen looked straight down to her feet, avoiding eye contact at all costs. Her voice began to break when responding, still staring at her boots below.

"Well, that's the thing, Nyx. I just needed to get away from James to at least tell someone about the situation. It's been six whole months and I haven't been able to tell a single person, I've been isolated all this time, right... look." Nyx looked at her with true concern - *what on Earth could have happened?* He placed his hand on her shoulder looking down at her.

"What happened Ellen?" For a brief moment, Ellen looked back up at Nyx to reveal tear drops sitting in her eyes, ready to stream down her face. She looked back down.

"I- I lied to James about mum." Nyx now understood her situation and how hard Ellen's life must have been before arriving in Zelpha. The tears released, streaming down her face. Dripping onto the boots she had been staring at this whole time.

~THE SECRETS OF ZELPHA~

"Our mum is gone. She passed away six months ago, I've been alone for so long, and now all these people- and James - it's-" Nyx interrupted her distress with a hug. Almost running at her from the few steps away he had been standing. She rested her head on his chest and looked up at him.

"I don't know what to say, I'm scared." Nyx would not let go of this hug, wanting Ellen to feel safe... and not alone, for once. She kept her head on his chest, and her eyes gazing up at him.

"It's okay, you've told someone. I'll help you, for now; let's not have him worrying and have a look at the village, it will all be sorted soon, don't worry." Ellen's tears were wiped away by Nyx and they both gave each other a small smile - fake or not, this was a big thing for Ellen at that moment. She reached into her back pocket, where an envelope lay, *was it time?*

"I really hope this resolves soon, I can't let him keep thinking mums here and all is good, but I also can't... let's just go and look at the village again."

Ellen - who was no longer crying, and Nyx had rushed their way back into the room where James was writing, with his head on the desk.

"James!" Nyx shouted, running in. James woke up from his sleepy mess, startled.

"Agh! Nyx, calm down" he shouted with fright. Jolting up from the desk. He turned and looked around, the first thing he noticed was that Ellen looked a little more pale than usual, yet still held her goofball-like smile.

"We found them!" she shouted at James who was still half asleep. Although his body was alert, his mind was still ready for his nap. He gave Ellen a questioning look, *who have they found?*

"The magical creatures, they don't seem like dragons and unicorns to me." Nyx joked. The group laughed until James' curiosity got the better of him.

"Oh, describe them!" he requested with excitement and wonder.

"I drew a sketch, hence why we took so long." Nyx put his arm around Ellen to comfort her as they both knew the true reason for their delay. His other hand reached into his back pocket to get the paper for James to see until their conversation was disturbed by Gak's voice from afar, calling for them to come to him.

"Grab everything and put it in my room, we can carry on another time!" Said Nyx. With this, the three started picking all bits of paper and books from the desk ahead - putting them in their pockets and in the bag Nyx had used to pack his things for his stay at the castle.

After their evening meal and finishing off some of their work, Gak entered the room.

~THE SECRETS OF ZELPHA~

"Right, Ellen, James, I think it's time for you two to go back." James' sweet rosy face was replaced with a shaken pale figure. All colour had left him, even his eyes faded a little.

"Wait, do you think we will be allowed back sometime?" he asked quickly after hearing this information. He had to stay, he had to reveal the secrets that had been surrounding him this past year - he had missed his only opportunity. From head to toe, James was filled with worry and guilt. He could have finally resolved the secrets of Zelpha, yet spent his time where all the knowledge of this dimension was surrounding him, working on some stupid book.

That was it, Ellen and James were taken back to the school where no information on the world, its history, or their exit could be revealed.

~13~
RELEASE OF SECRETS

Ellen and James had made their beds. She sat on her bed with her knees to her chest, her head gently resting on her shoulder.

"That was quite the day wasn't it..." Ellen commented. She sighed from exhaustion, her day couldn't go on much longer. James had a single laugh to himself before responding.

"It sure was." he now turned around to sit on his freshly made bed and continued, "We've had too much new information honestly." Ellen brushed her multicoloured locks out of her face, now keeping her head up in an attempt to not fall asleep. She looked at the boy sitting beside her and let out another sigh.

"I just wish they'd let us in the castle for one more day, that way we could definitely clear up some things in this mess!" she mumbled as her head hit her arms again.

"Yes," James agreed, "That way we'd also get to go home..." Ellen's head automatically jolted up at that comment, her tired expression sunk and faded down. She shoved the heel of her hand into her face followed up by a fake yawn.

~THE SECRETS OF ZELPHA~

"What's happening Ellen?" he asked with true concern, something wasn't right beneath the blanket of secrets she was holding. Her hands started to tremble, the blanket began to fall.

"What do you mean? Nothing is happening." He sighed and looked at the girl who was trying to hold all of her secrets together like a large pile of jam jars.

"I know something is wrong at home." James pushed with a need to know. What world would he be going back to? What could have happened?

"No, what do you mean? Nothing is wrong!" Ellen fired back. Holding onto all of these secrets was very stressful, they were about to go flying all over the stone-cold room. It was with that comment that James realised that this was no longer small talk, this was turning into an argument. A proper argument with his sibling. His loving side faded, he needed to know what was happening at home. With a slightly raised voice, he began responding,

"Ellen, just tell me! I know that there is an issue! Why won't you tell me?" Ellen was really holding back the tears now. She didn't want an argument but this was the moment when she realised she had no escape from it, she had to start revealing the truth. Letting her secrets free. She went to speak but realised, that if she spoke she was going to cry. She would break. There was no other option, so while trying to hold back her tears as best as possible she said,

~THE SECRETS OF ZELPHA~

"It's just that mum's health has been getting slightly worse, that's all!" James knew this wasn't the whole truth. What was keeping her from showing her true colours around her brother? He was her only family left.

"Just tell me the whole truth! Tell me, is she gone?" Ellen stared at him, so many emotions were running through her mind, that she didn't know how to respond. Blank-faced, she stared at him, until she came back to the present moment and blatantly lied.

"What? What, n-no!" This had James angry, she was never a liar. Why now?

"Is she gone? Tell me the truth, I have the right to know just spit it out!" Ellen burst into tears, dropping her blanket, dropping all of those jam jars. She could no longer protect her brother from the truth.

"Fine. Yes, she's gone! She's been gone for over six months!" she went to give him a hug and try to end this argument. That was not in James' plan. He reacted in the last way she expected him to. Automatically, he blamed himself.

"This is all my fault, isn't it? It's because I left home. Why have I done this?! It's all my fault. I need to put this right." and with that, the boy was off. He went running as far as he possibly could, as fast as his legs would allow him, slamming the door shut behind him. She wailed in mental and physical pain. She had lost her mother, and now it seemed like her brother didn't even love her.

~THE SECRETS OF ZELPHA~

"I can't leave him by himself," she cried as she bashed the door open and began chasing after him. "James! Where are you going?" she questioned in a hushed urgent tone, hoping not to wake anyone up. She continued to chase after him as he ignored her repeatedly. Until the pair stopped running. He turned to her and shouted.

"I don't care! I'm getting us out of this weird world with these weird people!" and with that he ran, off once again, into a corridor on the teacher's side of the school.

"Weird people? They are your friends!" Ellen shouted back. They continued to run in silence until they reached the castle grounds. He went to run to a bookcase as Nyx entered the room mid-yawn.

"What is all this noise-" he spotted the two in front of him. "What are you two doing?" he shouted at the two. James shushed Nyx and continued to go to the bookshelf. Ellen rolled her eyes at James' response and gave Nyx little to no explanation.

"I don't know, just keep quiet." James decided it was only fair that Nyx understood what was going on, although he wanted to do this independently. He required no help. He needed nobody, or so he thought.

"I am looking for this book," he explained to the two. Ellen got closer to James, more annoyed than ever now. She knew this had a much deeper meaning then a book.

"Is that really what all of this is about?" she asked only slightly, trying to hide her fury.

~THE SECRETS OF ZELPHA~

"I am going home," he stated without even looking at his sister's face. He had absolutely no interest in what the others were going through. To them, this comment made little to no sense. Footsteps approached the scene. The first to recognise who the footsteps belonged to was Nyx.

"Quick! Hide!" he whispered at the two as a warning. Ellen, James and Nyx hid behind an unused staircase as Ms Gaunt and Gak unlocked the castle's front gate, relocking it behind them. She held Gaks wrist with a mischievous smile, dragging him through the room.

"You're pushing your luck... kid." she laughed at her own comment like she was the greatest comedian ever. Unlike the woman, Gak didn't find it so funny. Gak looked down at his feet, continuing to be dragged by the woman, whose bun looked tighter at every glance.

"I'm sorry, I'll be better I promise," he clearly did not want to say that. Just like Ellen, Gak was soon to break.

"You will be better or I'll get you in those jails right away," she instructed. Gak's head stayed low as he mumbled

"You're the one without magic, not me" The three students stood in shock and horror. It wasn't allowed to be non-magical here, yet Ms Gaunt had managed it for years, with Gak knowing too! The one who seemed to resent her the most. He looked up to see the powerless monster staring at him, she was infuriated. He just let another secret go. As soon as he looked up he regretted his comment as he was fully sure she'd heard him.

"It seems like you want to go there right now." Ms Gaunt responded. The students stared in curiosity. Where was Gak going to be sent, knowing Ms Gaunt, it was surely nowhere particularly good. Gak broke. He couldn't take this life any longer. The release of secrets.

"In all honesty, it's better being with my sister, my own twin sister, than being controlled by a crazy woman!" Ellen looked at the two teammates as Nyx whispered something along the lines of 'the group', and James whispered something about a girl, a girl called 'Aria'. Ms Gaunt was certainly not happy. Crazy woman, twin sister, Ms Gaunt was having none of this. "Crazy woman eh? You're the one stuck in a kid's body!" she shouted another secret for the dimension of Zelpha to hear. Ellen, James and Nyx looked at each other while each of their faces contained pure fear. *'Child's body' What the hell was going on?*

"That's it for you 'young boy'..." Ms Gaunt started laughing again. It all made sense, the 'young boy' and 'kid' comments. Gak was no 'young teacher' he was a usual teacher, stuck in his younger self.

"Fine! Perfectly fine by me!" Gak needed something, he had needed it for many years. Today was the day when he was going to get what he truly needed. Holding his wrist tighter - to the point a red mark, or maybe even cut skin would be left

~THE SECRETS OF ZELPHA~

behind - she dragged him towards one particular turret of the castle, the one that led to the clocktower, she pointed at a trapdoor in the floor. Gaunt shoved Gak to the floor and started to unlock the gate.

~14~

FEAR AND CONFUSION

All of a sudden a non-human-like being appeared behind Ms Gaunt. Ellen and Nyx looked at each other instantly knowing what it was, it was a magical being, what were they doing here? Ms Gaunt had her back to it until it punched her from behind. She jumped - believing she and Gak had been alone - and turned to face it. A few more magical beings appeared and blocked the exit way of the turret Ms Gaunt and Gak were standing in.

"Hello there." the second being smiled, and slightly tilted its head to the left. Ms Gaunt was not happy, this magical being was on her property when she had business to deal with, and she was not going to be allowing this.

"Who are you? What are you doing here?" she shouted with pure anger at the small being that stood ahead of her. The one that had previously hit Ms Gaunt responded.

~THE SECRETS OF ZELPHA~

"We're from the village. You know that place you forced us to stay." Ms Gaunt argued back, denying that she had ever done such things.

"Really? Then I suppose you'll have no problem sharing the castle then!" The second being responded. The colour missing from Gak's face slowly started to reappear, yet he still seemed unhappy. The three students looked at each other in fear, wondering what they should do.

"We can't allow them to do this to us," Ellen whispered in fear. Nyx put his arm around Ellen, hoping to comfort her. Yet James responded with something not so comforting.

"I have to go over there." He whispered without even thinking. Nearly blowing their hiding spot, they had no plan, Ellen wouldn't allow that. She grabbed his wrist and pulled him back to their hiding spot. This was when they began to formulate their plan. James - who had been at the school much longer than the others - explained the school concept of magic alarms, they would have magic alarm drills for safety purposes. He began explaining the magical alarms go off if someone uses magic to harm someone else, and then everyone must evacuate through the castle. If they found a way of setting off the magic alarms, each student and teacher would go through the castle grounds, giving everyone some form of safety. Ellen knew what she had to do, she nodded at Nyx as though he had just read her mind. Nyx nodded back. Ellen hesitated, this could be the end of her, she took a big breath in and thought *this is for mum*. She then strolled out of her hiding space, trying to look controlled and happy to be there. She stood behind the magical beings who had threatened Ms Gaunt and Gak.

"If you want the castle you'll have to fight me!" Ellen shouted at them. They responded by laughing a ridiculous amount, almost like her power was nowhere near being able to defeat theirs.

James realised what was going on and for the first time, Nyx saw what it was like for James to be truly petrified. James went to run out and get Ellen, but Nyx put his arm around him. Trying to comfort him, knowing that they had a plan.

"Really, you?" The first magical being said to her, not scared by her comment at all. Ms Gaunt saw Ellen and tried to hide her anger, after all, Ellen got them away from her.

"Ellen what on Earth are you-" She tried to take control of the situation but the magical beings had lost all interest in Ms Gaunt and Gak, and began talking over the two, like they weren't behind them at all!

"What are you talking about little girl? You really think you can beat us?" it screamed in her face. It began to walk over to Ellen, who was petrified but still stood tall, standing her ground.

"You sure are cocky for being so weak. I mean what can you even do to me?" it asked, laughing.

"I can fight you!" she screamed, causing an echo to bounce off the walls. Gak, now very concerned for Ellen, shouted at her.

~THE SECRETS OF ZELPHA~

"Ellen! What are you doing?" The magical beings had enough of Ms Gaunt and Gak talking, the magical beings tied their legs together and their hands behind their backs with some invisible magic rope, making them stay quiet. Ellen and the magical being argued back and forth until it had enough.

"Fight me, you idiot!" Ellen screamed directly in its face full of fury.

"Idiot?! How dare you call ME, as a superior creature to YOU, an- an IDIOT!" On 'idiot' the magical being put all of its focus into Ellen's body. Furthermore, throwing her against the wall using its powers, Ellen was in agony, she could hardly move. However, her plan had worked. *James and Nyx will be safe.* She thought smiling through the pain, with the magic alarms ringing what seemed to be throughout her entire body.

Fear bombarded James' entire soul. He never lets anyone hurt his sister, but this time it was his own fault. He should have gone out there, he should have set off the alarms but now he was looking down at the girl whimpering in pain. All these thoughts flew at James in less than a second, until he quickly screamed.

"Ellen!" he ran from his hiding spot over to her. This left the two imprisoned teachers shaken. More magical beings started to flood the castle, destroying everything in their way.

"I'm fine, protect yourself." Ellen tried to reply back but was in too much pain to shout. While saying this she attempted to lift herself up, resulting in another crash to the floor. James, who had now reached Ellen responded.

~THE SECRETS OF ZELPHA~

"No, I'm helping you, it's the least I can do after earlier." The way James had hurt Ellen finally hit him, as he and Nyx got her up. She had been alone for months, and now finally reunited with her family, she was knocked down. Knocked down so far she could no longer stand independently. Ellen wrapped her arms over James' shoulder and he lifted her from the ground.

"James you get Ellen sorted, I found out where Gak keeps his weaponry, we have to kill them all. Quickly." Nyx instructed, and James did as he was told. He ran with Ellen on his back to safety, to save his near-dead sister. He carried her up to the room where they had written the book about the magical beings earlier that day, the very magical beings that caused her to be in this pain. Ellen whimpered as James rested her on the table. He rushed around the room and found some form of first aid box. He had little knowledge in overworld first aid, let alone magical first aid; he didn't let Ellen know that though. He frantically rummaged through the box, trying to find something useful. The more he panicked, the more Ellen's fear began to grow.

"You're gonna be okay, I promise," James reassured her, continuing to search through the box. She laughed, she didn't want her last moments with her brother to be negative. She was quite literally dying and that was not for James' knowledge.

"I know you don't know what you're doing, don't lie," she said with a small smile. Ellen looked down at the boy who was on his knees, knowing her life lay in his hands. Would he save her? He was fumbling through the box, chucking things out

~THE SECRETS OF ZELPHA~

of it. A tear ran down her cheek, he would have no family left. James would have nobody. She didn't want him to live through the pain she had done, she had to survive this. Suddenly, Ellen's life was made to continue on a little longer as James handed her a green crystal labelled 'one-time healer'.

"Use this on your leg," he instructed the girl above her. They both smiled in relief as Ellen stood up independently, James still shot up to support any falls. He looked down at her.

"See? You can use magic. I knew you could do it," James said with a smile. Trying to cheer her up. She knew the two couldn't stay here, and hide from the world. If they were together, they may as well have an adventure! Watch all the secrets released. She slipped the crystal into the pocket of her trousers.

"We need to go!" Ellen told him. With the response of a nod, they both ran out of the room down the stairs back to the castle grounds, as more students began to enter, realising what was wrong. The two panicked, looking around for Nyx; they caught eye on Ms Gaunt. She was directing all of the students to a small trapdoor on the floor.

"The Deathstone Jails! Everyone go, now!" she shouted at the top of her lungs. As she did this, Mr Gallo and Ms Gaunt pulled out two swords dripping in an unknown grey magical substance protecting the entrance to the turret that the trapdoor was located in, not allowing magical beings to enter the jails.

~THE SECRETS OF ZELPHA~

Mr Gallo - the man who would protect his students with his life - ran to Ms Gaunt, shouting instructions.

"Kids, get yourself in the jails, quick! I'll protect you," he said, slashing his sword in all directions; looking around to make sure all the students were getting to safety. He pushed all of his black-grey hair out of his face; sweating in distress.

Ellen looked around her - bodies submerged in fear, and so was hers. Someone had to be strong here, or they would lose. She took a deep breath and tried to think of something positive; her mother. Her mother helped her through the depths of poverty, keeping the family together, and being strong. Her mother was strong. She had to be just like her, for her friends and most importantly, her brother.

Turning to face the other turret, she saw Nyx holding a collection of swords with the same dripping substance on the end of it but this time - it was blue. Ellen realised that the colour of the person holding it was the colour of their team. She rushed over to Nyx, gave one sword to James and gripped a weapon in each of her hands. Then, she turned to Mr Gallo.

"Sir! We are here to help," Ellen shouted at the tired, sweaty teacher ahead of her. As she spoke, her strength began to build. Mr Gallo stood with appreciation with the rest of the blue team, who were now all holding their weapons. Ellen, whose mind was in a different dimension, suddenly heard Dusk's voice,

"They're flooding into the school and all over the castle; you can't do this alone."

~THE SECRETS OF ZELPHA~

Gale squeezed his eyes shut and transformed into a small-sized lion, yellow all over with a pink strip of fur over his head, representing his pink hair in human-form. He roared at a magical being and put it in his mouth with one bite; instantly gagging straight after while turning back into his human form.

As this was ongoing Coverly was putting her focus on several magical beings and throwing them into the ceiling with all her force.

James - an already overprotective older brother - was not in need of any help, all he needed was his friends to get to safety. *I called them weird people, I have to protect them.* He thought to himself.

"Guys! You need to get yourself safe! Go!" he shouted to them whilst continuing to kill all the beings nearby.

Ellen could clearly see what was going on in James' mind. He was in mortal danger, everyone here was taking the initiative to take leadership, to care for all besides themselves.

As the group started to head to the jails, Reid realised James wasn't following on.

"James, are you not coming with us?" she asked concerned for her friend. James, who still refused to look away from the crowd of magical beings, shouted back; in hopes of being heard in the loud crowded room.

"I've got to keep you all safe, don't worry I'll meet you down there!" These could be their last moments, and James didn't turn his head at all. He needed to make sure that this wasn't their last moment, he saw it as his responsibility to keep them safe. Ellen continued to rush the groups out of the castle and went back to fighting without knowing Dusk hadn't left.

Dusk thought they were about to lose, about to die. She wouldn't see her friends or family again; she instantly ran to Evelyn for her last moments.

"Evelyn! Come on. We need to get to safety." she said in the hope that she would finally talk to her again. Evelyn took a moment, blew up a magical being and grabbed Dusk's hand. She stayed silent, breaking Dusk's heart that she wouldn't talk during their possible last moments, but she stayed strong, holding her hand tight.

Myrtle ran into the room with a sword dripping in dark red melted crystal. The sword itself was grey; with a blue ribbon tied tighter than you could imagine around the handle. In her other hand, she held a collection of multicoloured crystals, in all different shapes and sizes. Each crystal, attached to a thin necklace chain.

"Well, you're going to need more than the five of you. Ellen, get here." Myrtle shouted. With no trust in Myrtle, Ellen didn't turn to look at her, or what she was holding.

"It's not time for your games," Ellen mumbled to herself. Myrtle moved her eyes from Ellen, closer to her feet. With one crystal brighter than the others, Ellen moved from her original spot closer to Myrtle. Oblivious to the fact she was moved via magic Ellen turned and scolded Myrtle,

~THE SECRETS OF ZELPHA~

"What? I need to protect them!" Myrtle placed her hand on Ellen's wrist and looked at her with true sincerity, something Ellen had never seen from the girl before.

"I understand that. I am here to help you, Ellen." Myrtle opened up her hand to reveal the glow trapped within it - crystals. Ellen went to argue back until she looked down at the items in her hand. She had been stopped.

"All these years, I thought I needed these... but now I know it was not for me, but for you." she looked down at her hand, talking quite quietly, yet Ellen still heard and understood what had to be done. Myrtle put the crystals in Ellen's hand, Ellen attached them to her necklace and took a deep breath. She turned away from Myrtle, Ellen's fear of magic was heightened higher than ever. She looked ahead and saw that Nyx and James were hurt and defeated, whilst trying to kill the beings ahead of them. Nyx turned to defeat one behind him and saw the crystals glow on Ellen's necklace. He was aware she had a fear of magic he shouted at her,

"Come on Ellen, you've got this!" Life or death, family or death, friends or death, she could not pick death. As she was about to start using magic Mr Gallo was ushering them to the jails. The three followed him, with magical beings chasing not long after. All three had fallen through this trapdoor and landed on top of each other in a dark room. James realised what was going on in this room and blurted out in annoyance. This was a maze.

~THE SECRETS OF ZELPHA~

"You have gotta be kidding me right now, I suck at these!" he whined, scared for his life. Ellen, who had been quiet the whole time spoke, very calmly.

"It's this way." realising the two members were looking at her in confusion, looking for an explanation, she had to follow up with. "I have a feeling." Knowing they had nothing to lose, they followed her. As she spoke, another crystal glowed.

"I'll kill them off behind," James informed them. As he said this Mr Gallo fell from the trapdoor. He grabbed his back, wincing in pain.

"There is no chance I'm letting you do that." Mr Gallo stood behind the group as Ellen led the way. Whilst walking, Mr Gallo held his sword tightly in his hand.

As Mr Gallo and the three students made their way through the maze - being followed by magical beings, Gak ran to a specific cell while screaming so loud the four could nearly hear him from the maze.

"Aria!" As he said this a girl dived at him into a hug. Ellen, James, Nyx and Mr Gallo rushed into the cell and looked at the mass of people ahead of them, assessing the situation and their options. That's until Mr Gallo caught the eye of Gak with this girl. A tear fell from his eyes, with a mixed message on his face; happiness and guilt as he watched the girl wail in joy.

"Gak, I-I can't believe it's really you!" she shouted "It's been so long!" suddenly her happy mood faded, turning exasperated. "Where is that witch? I am going to kill her for

~THE SECRETS OF ZELPHA~

what she's put us through" Ellen observed them having their conversation with pure confusion on her face, who was this girl? Why did she know Gak? And who was this witch she speaks of?

"Leave her alone, I don't want to waste any more of my time, now that I am finally with my sister once again." This shocked Ellen. Gak has a sister? How was it only now she was discovering this? And how on Earth was she here?

The siblings' re-bonding continued on in the background as Ellen, James, Nyx and Mr Gallo looked at each other wondering what to do. It wouldn't be long until the magical beings caught up to the group. Mr Gallo scanned the room for Ms Gaunt and saw her enter the jail-like cell below him.

The four of them went down some steps to get to the other people, including Gak and his sister. The conversation between the twins was back at the forefront of Ellen's mind. She looked over at Aria and listened in,

"Oh my, it feels like I've been waiting here forever, I had two options: wait for you or death. I was so close to falling down there, but I didn't. I stayed as long as I could." this girl had been stuck in here this whole time, what? *This was insane.* Ellen thought to herself.

"I love you so much for that, you're so strong. You knew I'd find my way back to you. I've tried so hard!" Gak responded by holding the girl tighter. This was when Ellen realised, the girl

~THE SECRETS OF ZELPHA~

said 'falling down there'. She walked over to an archway at the end of Aria's cell and examined the jails.

The jails were described as hell, people were once sent to them for being non-magical but a few years back that changed, they became for the winners of The Games who Ms Gaunt wouldn't allow home - such as Aria. The jails were always freezing due to the sheer size of the place, it was always described as a cruel and miserable place to be stuck in. No matter how you looked at it, there was no good factor. The jails were known for being somewhere you couldn't escape. This was because the cells were hundreds of metres below ground, the only way out was death.

Having a few moments away from the battle, Ellen examined Aria's cell itself. A stone brick box - a few bricks infested with moss - minimal decoration and clearly she didn't have any of her own possessions on her when arriving. A grey bed, a table, and a small pile of books.

She refocused her attention on Gak as he loudly announced,

"Stay away and don't worry; I'm protecting all of the students... and Aria." Aria stared at Gak with a proud look before hugging him tighter. Gak glanced down at her before looking back up. Letting go of Aria, he walked in front of the students and stared at the entranceway scouring for any of the magical beings. He could hear some of the students stifling their sobs, some were whispering to console them; while other students were pacing back and forth trying to keep themselves busy. A few students walked a bit closer to Gak and Aria to get a look at the entrance while also trying to stay protected.

"I love you so much," Aria spoke softly towards her brother before looking forward.

As they waited in fear, some of the students were shushing the others - Gak looked back to see some of the older students holding a hand over some of the younger one's mouths. Mr Gallo stepped forward,

"Everyone get as far back into the jails as possible!" He shouted. Ellen, James, Nyx and Mr Gallo then went past Gak and Aria and helped move some students towards the back of the jail.

"I'm scared." Ellen heard a girl named Paige whimper in a hushed, crackly voice.

"It's okay, get as far back as you can." her team teacher, Mx Baire consoled and started to push her towards her other teammates.

Seeing this, other students huddled closer towards their teacher and teammates. They talked quietly with their teacher and friends while waiting for anything to happen.

"The beings are stupid, they can't get through the maze, so what's the plan?" Ellen stated.

Ms Gaunt rushed over to all of those in the jail cell closest to the entrance,

~THE SECRETS OF ZELPHA~

"Stand as close to the back as possible. Hopefully, they will fall through the exit and die."

"Stay here, they'll look after you. I have to go and help!" Gak said to Aria as he began to turn around she grabbed his hand and shouted at him.

"No! You can't go, it's too dangerous. I have only just gotten you back, after all this time I can't have my brother taken away from me again." Pleading him to stay, Aria held his hand as tight as she could.

Gak placed his hand on top of Aria's, in a reassuring way. With the calmest and most serious voice he could hold, he spoke looking into her teary eyes.

"I need to. I'll be back, I promise." With that Gak let go of Aria's hand and started to run towards the scene, getting closer to Ms Gaunt. "Ms Gaunt allow powers in the jails quickly!" Ms Gaunt's face filled with fear, she was not prepared for a fight without her crystals.

"I can't! I don't control it, just take all the weapons you can find, and without their magic - they're weak." Gaunt stated in a shaky voice.

Everyone fell silent before scurrying to their weapons. As they were running around, grabbing weapons the enemy finally arrived. Ellen, James, and Nyx saw five figures emerge from the shadows and into the corridor. The teachers walked in front of the children to protect them, and Ms Gaunt walked in front of her teachers.

~THE SECRETS OF ZELPHA~

"Why can't we use magic, you witch!" It yelled in a shrill voice towards Ms Gaunt.

Gak saw that Ms Gaunt was shaking, be it fear or anger - he did not know.

"The jails just do that, we can't control it," responded Ms Gaunt in a worried tone.

"Give us our powers back!" Another demanded.

As Gak was moving forward his facial expression began to change to a look of frustration as he moved closer to the magical beings he began to raise his voice.

"She said she can't, have you got an issue with that?" Ellen started to get more and more frustrated with the situation that was happening in front of her and began to yell at everyone,

"Ugh just get this over and done with!" She had a hint of anger in her tone. After she shouted, Ellen realised that the magical beings were distracted and she decided to use this as an opening to kick the magical beings as hard as she could out of the cell into the voice below. The being began to understand what was happening and shouted to Ellen.

"You little brat." The being now had a tone that was angrier than before.

"Why are we the only ones fighting? Come over here!" The magical being instructed to all of the other beings. As they all rushed into the room a few fell out of the cell - to their deaths - due to the cramped space.

~THE SECRETS OF ZELPHA~

"They are CHILDREN, there's nothing to be afraid of!" Another being shouted at them all.

James, now confident as they were all agitated, looked at Ellen and smiled.

"Well Ellen, you seem to have started something here." He giggled.

"Yeah, let's go finish this." She responded with just as much confidence. Both their swords glowed brighter.

James jumped off the edge of the jail cell, falling and crying in fear that his death was upon him, that his magic wouldn't work. He then used his magic crystal to switch places with a magical being causing it to die from the fall. That was until the crystal magic ran out and James was stuck on the jail floor and the dead body was rotting in the jail cell.

"Please help me!" James screamed as his voice echoed throughout the entire jail.

"Coverly! Get James, quick!" Ellen shouted petrified for her brother. Coverly ran towards the exit looking at the abyss hundreds of feet below. As she was not in a jail cell her powers could work, furthermore, she lifted him to safety and they both ran back into the cells.

Absolutely revolted by the dead body Nyx kicked it repeatedly until it fell out of the cell, splatting on the floor. As he turned he saw Ellen looking slightly zoned out, just staring at Gak.

~THE SECRETS OF ZELPHA~

"Come on Ellen! Now's not the time!" Nyx shouted at her. Ellen instantly pointed at a magical being who was behind Gak, holding a sword someone had dropped.

"It's going to stab you!" Ellen shouted at Gak. Gak turned around seeing a magical being begin to take out its sword, now prepared he kicked it into the void below.

"Woah, Ellen? James? What was that? Without magic, how?" Gak asked with shock. He picked up the sword, giving himself a weapon.

"The crystals!" Ellen shouted in realisation. Although magic from the soul could not be used here, nobody spoke about magic from a crystal; as all were expected to be magical from the soul, it didn't need to be confirmed.

"You still have those?!" Gak blurted out, his skin now paper white. His magic, his magic had been retrieved. After all these years Ellen had found it. But how?

"I gave her them!" Myrtle shouted loudly, with her sword in front of her face ready to protect herself. Everyone looked over to Myrtle in pure and utter shock. Why would someone with such a cold heart do something so warm and kind? Laryse was the most shocked, after all this time of backing Myrtle up she realised she didn't know anything about her.

"What? I thought you hated her?!" Laryse asked with anger in her tone. She left slightly more shaken, however, she didn't know if this was from Myrtle, or the fact that she finally expressed her own emotions, not her 'friends'.

~THE SECRETS OF ZELPHA~

Crap Myrtle thought, she nearly let her secrets slip into the open, quick, think of something!

"I do! We're in the middle of like, a war! She's just more useful this way!" Myrtle argued back in her usual mean voice.

James noticed that an argument was breaking out between the two. *Ugh, again really. Not now!* He thought. He knew he had to put a stop and get them to continue thinking about the ongoing situation, not whatever their petty argument was over this time.

"It doesn't matter right now!" He argued back at them both, they looked at the ongoing battle and both realised how ridiculous they had been.

Ellen noticed a cell was empty, except from one magical being. She ran over to the cell it was in. By the time she reached the cell on the other side of the jails, she noticed, the was the only survivor - the one that had been here this entire time. The strongest. They were alone. Ellen's life was under threat once again, she was praying that her magic would become natural again.

"You just think you're such a good kid." it laughed to itself with self-confidence. It then finally realised, Ellen's face was not drowning in the fear it expected her to have. She looked... unphased.

"Yeah actually I do, I'm protecting my friends from monsters!" Ellen shouted back, hiding her fear.

~THE SECRETS OF ZELPHA~

"Is that what they told you we are? Monsters... MONSTERS?!" It shouted at her, it knew the magical being population was disliked by the more modern generation but certainly not that much.

"Yeah, and considering what you're doing I think you are!" She shouted back, her fear completely replaced by anger and her sword held high.

"I bet they didn't tell you that we were here first!" Ellen had now stopped listening, she was preparing to kill. "That they forced us into that village? You better stop now kid or you're going to get hurt-"

CRASH!
The being had dropped dead to the floor, with Ellen's blue crystal-infected sword lingering inside its body. Ellen instantly fell to the ground panting, letting her true emotion out. As tears flooded out her eyes, she realised - they had won.

~15~

THE FINAL GOODBYE

"Is... is everyone okay?" Ellen said, panting. Her hair was messy and her face was one of concern and worry for her friends. She looked at her surroundings, trying to spot everyone. "We... WE DID IT!" Ellen exclaimed, smiling brightly as she saw their victory coming up ahead. She looked at James, who was running over to her. As soon as everyone else saw James running, they followed along.

"Jane. Why?" Aria said, turning around to face Ms Gaunt with sheer anger in her voice. Her expression was full of resentment. She stared at Ms Gaunt with the same expression, waiting for her answer that she had spent years to find.

"What?" Ms Gaunt wanted to avoid the topic, she knew what she had done was wrong but she wasn't comfortable admitting the truth just yet.

"You left me in that jail for years... YEARS. At least Gak wasn't stuck there, but you KNEW I was there and yet you did nothing." Aria spoke as tears flooded her eyes and ran down her

~THE SECRETS OF ZELPHA~

face. This encounter with Ms Gaunt made her emotions run all over the place.

"Listen, we'll talk about this later. For now, let's get out of jail before anything else happens. Gak, check that the students are not injured so they can get out." Ms Gaunt instructed, with that same blank expression on her face.

"On it Ms Gaunt," Gak said, walking out and checking up on everyone. He asked the students how they were and made sure everyone was okay and didn't have any severe injuries. After a short while, all of the teachers and students made their way back through the maze with Ms Gaunt as their lead. When they saw the hole leading up to the ceiling they all started to mutter to one another trying to find a way out. As Gak tried to climb his way up, Coverly rushed over to him.

"I can give you guys a boost if needed. My magic does make me able to levitate people." Coverly spoke with a small smile on her face as she had just found their way out of the jails. She looked at Gak, who was thinking about a way out.

"Yes please. There's no other way out." Gak said, nodding. One by one Coverly levitated each student and teacher out of the jail into the castle grounds. That was until there were only two students left - Ellen and James. She moved her long blonde hair out of her face to see them both looking quite distant and upset.

"Ellen, James - you coming?" she asked cautiously, sympathising with how they felt after being in such danger. She

~THE SECRETS OF ZELPHA~

was sure they needed a moment to recover from their fear. Ellen looked up from the floor to Coverly who was standing near the exit.

"Let- let me and James have some time to ourselves first," she responded softly, not knowing what to say to her. Ellen turned her head to her brother and told him that she needed to talk to him, alone.

"Alright, but let me know when the two of you are ready, okay?" Coverly asked, calmly. She didn't want to upset them, as they clearly had many secrets hidden in their hearts.

As Coverly left the room Ellen grabbed James' wrist, bringing him closer to her. She didn't know how to word her emotions. It was that that made her realise that she couldn't start with her emotions, she had to explain the story - why they had to live this life, this horrible life.

"After you disappeared, for months and months we searched for you. Mum's mental and physical health started to deteriorate from staying up all day and night, searching the woods for you. Even Chester went missing for a bit." She started with. Although this was difficult for Ellen, he needed to hear the story after the night of the storm.

"What?" James responded he had only just realised it couldn't have been as simple as 'mother is dead' there had to be a story to it. Immediately he began to blame himself, thinking of the very few times he and his mother had argued or had bad days and how it could have led to her death. He had to know how she passed.

"Mum kept on getting worse and worse after we thought you were gone forever. I- I tried to look after her James, I really did. I tried so hard, but I'm just one person. Our mother is dead, and it's all my fault." With that Ellen burst into tears, she couldn't hide her emotions anymore. She had to be her true self. As she did this, James bent down and squished her into a hug, so tight it could have pushed out more tears from her eyes. He didn't let go as she couldn't see his face. However, you could see the brokenness within his eyes and the tears that fell from them.

The two siblings had a family that was held close together by their mother. Their mother was the superglue of the family. Over the past year, both of the siblings had learnt that life was nothing without family, and losing a member of the small family... was like losing a piece of their heart and soul. Continuing to hold his sister tight, James strengthened his voice enough to talk.

"Ellen, it was never your fault." he wiped the tears from his eyes and let go of the hug, tightly gripping her arms with his hands and looking into her hurt and broken eyes. "It... it stings that you kept this from me, but looking back I guess there really wasn't a great time to tell me. Considering I was too bubbly about seeing you." He tried to keep eye contact with his sister, but after knowing it was his fault a tear dropped from his eye.

~THE SECRETS OF ZELPHA~

    James had been too oblivious to even consider what his home life was like now, what Ellen had been through. He looked at the young girl in front of him and felt shame surrounding him, he hadn't even cared about her. All he wanted was for his sister to be okay, but in reality, he had never shown the emotion. How could she still love him after the way he had been? He had tried, yet it was still all his fault.

    Ellen looked back at her brother, feeling so sad that she was the one to tell him all of this, yet so proud that he was still by her side after hearing this news. He had supported her all her life and continued to do so during one of his most traumatic moments. Alongside blaming herself and believing that she was the cause of her mother's death - that she could still be here waiting for them to come home if she had tried a little harder - she was happy that she still had her brother by her side.

    James wiped the tears from his and his sisters eyes. They both gained the confidence to continue their conversation James decided to move away from the sad tone but stayed on topic.

    "Right, how will life work without mum at home?" he asked, now sitting on the stone-cold jail cell floor and leaning his back against the even colder wall. Ellen sat down next to him beginning to respond.

    "We can sort that out when we get to it. Knowing Ms Gaunt and her cold heart we won't be going anytime soon anyway," she responded by putting her arm around him. "I just want to say... I am really proud of you." James looked down at

~THE SECRETS OF ZELPHA~

his little sister with sheer confusion. After all he had caused, how could she be proud of him?

The two continued to talk about what life would be like when they eventually got home, where they would lay their mother to rest, and if Chester would be home - they spoke about everything and anything.

The conversation felt like it had lasted years. Eventually, James stood up from the floor and put a hand out to Ellen. She grabbed his hand pulling herself up from the cold stone she rested on. The two walked over to the maze trenching their way back through it. Reaching the centre of the maze - where they originally fell from - they spotted Coverly sitting on the floor waiting for them.

"Took your time, come on guys." She joked. She started to lift all three of them out of the maze back to the castle.

Ms Gaunt and Mr Gallo had agreed that everyone may stay at the castle grounds for a little while before going back to their day-to-day activities. She had a lot to sort out - why there was a hidden jail, why there were people in it, the list goes on.

When Ms Gaunt had realised Ellen and James were back to the surface she called for their attention. Looking sheepish, she asked to speak with the two students.

"If you want to go home, I think you have the right to do so. Tell the Ferryman you're the blue team. He will understand."

~THE SECRETS OF ZELPHA~

"The Ferryman?" James questioned, who was this 'Ferryman' and how would he get the two students home? No student at Zelpha had heard of a Ferryman.

"You know that empty boat when going to The Games?" Ms Gaunt began to explain who he was and how he would help them. "A man lives there, I actually have a bit of a story about him... anyway he will allow you back to Earth." The two looked at each other, realising they had never heard of a Ferryman or even seen him by the boat. What are the chances that he would have been away busy every time the students had a game? Something strange was going on here and James was determined to discover what it was.

"Oh? How did I now know this?" he asked with a face of sheer confusion.

"We don't tell the students mid-year, as we don't want them using it to escape immediately," she responded with a serious tone. *But why?* Ellen thought *Why do we have to stay here?* She looked around at the castle grounds realising the amount that had happened in the past few days, taking it in. She had travelled to a different dimension then made various friends from various dimensions then became magic then had a war then... then what? Then she just leaves, as simple as that. Then pretend it never happened?

"There are a few things I want to do before leaving," Ellen replied as James nodded in agreement and thanked Ms Gaunt for giving them information on the Ferryman.

~THE SECRETS OF ZELPHA~

"It's the least I can do after the pain I've caused," she responded looking down at the floor.

"Pain?" James questioned her. She may have been a bad person but she had never caused people any physical pain, had she? That's when James realised, he hadn't seen each cell of that jail - Aria wasn't the only one there.

"I'm sure you'll realise after speaking to people, I'll leave you both alone now. I am sorry," she responded looking into the eyes of the students with full sincerity. Ms Gaunt walked away, unable to look at the students anymore.

As Ms Gaunt left, Nyx spotted the two students standing there - dumbfounded.

"Ellen! James! Are you two okay?" Nyx asked rushing over to the two, they got slightly separated when the war was coming to an end. Ellen let Nyx know that they were okay until they looked over to James, seeing him looking quite down.

"I'm here if you need anything James, you know that," he said, placing a hand on James' shoulder. James responded with a forced smile.

"I actually wanted to talk about that... you being with us..." Ellen said kind of awkwardly, she hadn't thought this through yet or even asked James for that matter. "When we go home, do you have anyone to go to?" She understood that Ms Gaunt had included Nyx in being allowed to go home.

"In all honesty... I'm not entirely sure, I got here and I lost all of my memory of where I lived, who I lived with or well

~THE SECRETS OF ZELPHA~

anything... I'm not even 100% sure that I got my name correct..." he began to mumble, drowning in sadness. "However, something tells me I have nobody to go home to..."

Although Nyx had lost his memory, he had very strong senses about all sorts of things. His favourite colour, his name, if he had anyone to go home to. He may be wrong with all of these, however, it was a burning sensation that if he did not let it out into the world, then he would have no identity. James looked at the boy, he had no idea about what Nyx was going through all that time.

"Oh god! That must be awful, is there anything we can do?" he asked kindly. Unexpectedly, Nyx didn't have the chance to think of a response. Ellen was the one to respond.

"Yes, yes there is something we can do." She said looking at James. Now turning to Nyx she continued to ask. "Look Nyx, if you'd like to come home with us I'm sure it's okay with James and it's more than okay with me." Ellen realised she just asked him something that'd take a lot to process so she tried to lighten the mood. "Like what if James and I have *another* argument?" she ended sarcastically.

"It's a massive deal, I could have someone at home to go to, but also if I don't then I'll be homeless and alone."

Nyx looked slightly away, taking a moment to think clearly. He could be living a life of royalty or a life of misery, anything could await him. He could either take that risk or have a secure home, with friends to live with. Nyx began to think

~THE SECRETS OF ZELPHA~

about the person he had grown into while at Zelpha, both with those burning feelings and what had come naturally to him. He was happy with who he had become and part of what supported him in becoming this person was Ellen and James. He had made a decision.

"You know what, I'll take you up on that offer. Beats staying somewhere quiet in my opinion." Ellen jumped around bursting with excitement, unable to form a response.

"Don't worry, it'll barely be quiet at home with all three of us, particularly Ellen." James ended the conversation before the green and yellow teams walked over.

"Well, I guess we have to say goodbye to you guys," Yadira said being the first to talk, as she knew the second Bridget spoke she would burst into tears. However, it happened to be that as soon as anybody spoke Bridget would burst into tears, as that was exactly what she did.

Her words muffled by her tears, the young girl tried to speak to Ellen, James and Nyx.

"I-I I just can't believe it... th-the three of you are going..." and with that, Bridget shoved her head into the three standing blankly in front of her, trying to embrace them into a tight hug. She wailed and screamed, sobbing out "I'll miss you" and practically crushing them with her hugs. Her friends repeatedly asked her to calm down but nothing was stopping her sadness.

~THE SECRETS OF ZELPHA~

We've only been here for four days, thought Ellen, *How can she be this sad if she's only known us for such a short time?*

Bridget whined as Yadira peeled the girl off the three. She walked her over to the nearest wall, pouting, and continuing to cry. Although Bridget knew that she could be mature she found life so much more interesting when being childish and having fun. From time to time this would get her odd looks, all she wanted was to enjoy life but it seemed to be that nobody would take her seriously in times of importance because of it. In reality, although Bridget was sixteen, she was just a child at heart.

Now that Bridget had been dealt with, the other five were able to say their goodbyes more maturely. Coverly hugged Ellen, James, and Nyx individually, then spoke.

"Man, this is kinda sappy but I'm happy to see you guys go home. You deserve to be happy." Although they would no longer be at Zelpha with their friends, they'd be able to finally go back to their world. A world they had been waiting for so long to see once again.

"Yeah, but in all honesty, James, I'm glad you're leaving. I can finally eat my own food in peace." Gale added, arms folded looking serious. James knew he wasn't serious at all. Gale knew he would go hungry any day to make sure his best friend was well fed.

Playfully, James pushed Gale causing him to unfold his arms and start laughing. Gale - who had never been the hugging type - opened his arms wide for James to hug. He was left

~THE SECRETS OF ZELPHA~

smiling. The atmosphere was quite light, although it was somewhat sombre. If these would be their last few moments with the other people here, they wanted them to be filled with joy.

That was until Myrtle slowly entered the castle, creeping quietly and standing alone awkwardly. Everyone was focused elsewhere, laughing and joking with each other, so she decided to cough to grab the group's attention. The mood of the room dropped almost instantly and she received a few stares of disgust. Almost everyone seemed negatively affected, excluding Ellen, who took a step towards her to include her in the conversation.

"Oh, hey Myrtle," Ellen said politely. Myrtle took a breath to respond but she was quickly cut off by Nyx.

"What's she doing here?" He interrupted rather rudely. The group was repulsed by her presence; confused as to why she decided to even show her face. Bridget still wept in the corner a few metres away from them all, looking for someone to comfort her. Myrtle's eyes glanced between Bridget, Ellen, and the floor. She took a step closer to Ellen, but James and Nyx jumped forward to block her.

"Hey! I know you did something to her in those Games. You can back off!" James shouted. Myrtle retracted from the conversation slowly, untucking her hair to cover her face as she began to become teary. Nyx responded swiftly, not giving Myrtle time to speak.

~THE SECRETS OF ZELPHA~

"Get lost Myrtle, nobody wants you here." He said with hatred in his voice, Myrtle tried to speak whilst holding back her tears, her throat closing up.

"I just..." she looked down and began to turn and walk away. She lost all hope to even try and communicate with the other students since they wouldn't listen anyway.

Ellen thought about how Myrtle gave her those crystals earlier, and how those crystals saved everyone's lives. They had to talk. She had to thank her, that was the least she could do.

"It's fine, guys, give me a moment." Ellen requested calmly. If she didn't show that she was okay she knew the others would push Myrtle away.

"Not without me, with all she's done" James responded to Ellen without taking his eyes off the girl. Ellen tapped James on the shoulder to get his attention and level him a look.

"I'll be fine. I promise." James finally broke his eyesight off Myrtle and moved to Ellen. She had a trusting look on her face, but that didn't mean he trusted her. He thought hard for a moment before replying,

"You have exactly five minutes; then I am coming to get her." James didn't exactly trust Myrtle - why would he, she'd done nothing to earn it - but he trusted Ellen's judgement. He could give them a few minutes to talk if it was as important as Ellen made it to be.

"And he won't be alone." Nyx backed James' comment up. He puffed out his chest, trying his best to look intimidating

~THE SECRETS OF ZELPHA~

and keeping his eyes on Myrtle with a glare as cold as ice. It was clear he trusted Myrtle with Ellen as much as James did - which was to say he didn't trust her at all.

Ellen and Myrtle wandered a little further away from the group for a few seconds alone, with James' and Nyx's protective glares following behind. Ellen looked down at her feet and gave an apology to Myrtle for her friend's behaviour. She understood that they were only trying to protect her, but Myrtle was human too and deserved to be treated like one. Especially for everything she's done for them.

Myrtle accepted Ellen's apology. She paused for a second, not knowing what to say. Her hair covered her face as she looked down and away. Ellen opened her mouth to speak.
Before she could say anything, a tear had escaped from Myrtle's red, pain-filled eyes. It trailed only a few centimetres down her cheek before she wiped it away, but she wasn't quick enough for Ellen to ignore the glimmer of it in the castle lights. Concern instantly hit Ellen.

"What's up? Are you okay?" she questioned.
Myrtle still couldn't meet Ellen's gaze, and her feet began to wander as she stepped back and forth. Ellen waited a few seconds and then followed Myrtle when she paced over to a bookcase, further away from everyone. Ellen didn't stop following, still curious for a response and hoping the girl was okay. Myrtle sat down on the floor leaning against the range of books. The

~THE SECRETS OF ZELPHA~

blonde-haired girl was unsure of what she wanted to say to Ellen, or rather how much she wanted to say.

Myrtle reached a decision in her head and took a breath. She wasn't sure if it was the right decision, but if Ellen trusted her enough to be alone with her then she could trust her back. Looking into Ellen's eyes, Myrtle saw the hidden heartbreak. This week in Zelpha had changed her life, and it had clearly changed everyone else's lives too, considering how they were gathering together to spend time as friends. Ellen had kept so many secrets - why didn't all these people hate her? Isn't that what Myrtle had done?

Myrtle suddenly realised something. Ellen did keep secrets, but she was never rude to anyone. All her life she'd been taught that non-magical beings were evil and that they were disgusting, jealous creatures who begged, stole, borrowed, and bartered to have the same skills as those with magic did. Compared to all her years at Zelpha, these five days had taught her that the stereotype was false. That non-magical beings could be helpful, knew how to be polite, and were kind. Myrtle knew that James and Nyx knew about Ellen's lack of magic, and they probably didn't have any either. They were still people, regardless of whether they had magic or not. They were impolite to her, but she could understand why. Her point was that Ellen's secrets had been let out into the open, into the world. Whether it be one person or a whole magical school of people; her secrets were out there for good. Myrtle decided that it was time to stop letting hers weigh her down.

"It's just all this time," Myrtle began. Ellen tried to encourage her to continue with a soft smile, giving her the confidence to persist. Myrtle did her best to smile back. "I was doing stuff I shouldn't have done to get these crystals." she finished. An awkward delay followed. Ellen hummed and nodded to show Myrtle she was still paying attention. This secret was something that deeply affected Myrtle, and Ellen wouldn't want to make her feel unwelcome as the others did.

"You know, like, breaking the rules." Myrtle gulped, feeling pinned under Ellen's gaze. Her throat began to close up again, as though the tears were coming back.

"So I acted like I hated all of you, and it was a trap, I couldn't escape... I should have tried to be nice to everyone-" Myrtle rambled, her tone breaking as her voice box betrayed her. Ellen saw the gleam of light reflecting from her eyes, tears finally escaping. Ellen raised her arm to pat Myrtle on the shoulder comfortingly, but Myrtle spoke before she could.

"Now everybody just hates me!" Myrtle yelled, cupping her face in her hands - drowning herself in tears.

Ellen placed her arm around Myrtle, resting her head against Myrtle's shoulder in a half-hug. She finally understood why Myrtle had been so horrible all this time, her secrets finally being revealed.

~THE SECRETS OF ZELPHA~

Realising Ellen had shown affection - that she didn't hate her - Myrtle took her face out of her hands and looked at the girl who was still resting on her. Someone cared for her.

"I'm sure one day they'll get it, don't worry..." she stated, now turning to look at her. "You do know that James, Nyx and I are going home today though, right?" she asked, concerned for Myrtle. She couldn't comfort her forever.

The crying girl still felt too stunned to speak, as though the small act of kindness she had received had completely changed everything in her world. She quietly coughed, half trying to regain the confidence to speak to Ellen and half trying to clear her throat.

"Really? Well, I guess I'll just be stuck in this world with a bunch of people who hate me..." she responded, now instead staring at the ceiling above. She decided to try lightening the mood and wiped her tears away. Turning around, she saw Laryse and added "and that idiot" to the end of her sentence with a chuckle. The moment Myrtle pointed at Laryse, who had been trying to approach the two but not intrude on their emotional moment together, the girl knocked her arm against a bookshelf. Evidently not having Myrtle by her side was a little too much for her brain to handle. Myrtle and Ellen giggled together, until Ellen sighed, and grabbed the crystals that were wrapped around her neck. Myrtle now felt somewhat clearer after crying and telling Ellen her secret.

~THE SECRETS OF ZELPHA~

"I'll pass a message onto the group, to explain that you're not the vile person they think you are - that you're a really great person deep down." Before Ellen continued, she stood to her feet, wary of James and Nyx's glares possibly finding the two again. "Either way, do you want these crystals back?" Ellen asked, holding onto those that were still attached to her necklace. In reality, Myrtle had spent a long time working so hard for these, she deserved to keep them. Straight after Ellen, Myrtle got to her feet to answer her.

"Are you serious right now? You saved all of our lives. The least I can do is let you keep some stupid crystals in return." These crystals had ruined Myrtle's reputation in Zelpha, she certainly didn't want them. Either way, it was very clear to all that Ellen was from the Overworld - the dimension where no magic can be found - so it may make her life at home a little more interesting. People would have a good reason for calling her a witch, at least.

She thanked Ellen for offering to pass the message on to her group, they certainly wouldn't believe her but if it came from Ellen herself it may seem a little more genuine.

"Real friends will understand," Ellen responded, engulfing Myrtle in a hug. Myrtle realised that Ellen was a real friend. That she did care about her, not just her actions.

In the end, no apology could take back all that Myrtle had done to Ellen and her friends. Getting them into trouble, making them disliked by teachers, harming the mind of Evelyn,

~THE SECRETS OF ZELPHA~

making all of their lives a misery; however, her secrets were out now. It was up to them whether they would forgive her or not.

Feeling the warmth of Ellen's hug made Myrtle's hands shake as she held her. It caused Myrtle to experience a feeling she hadn't felt for a long time, such a long time it took a while for her to recall which feeling it was - love. Ellen pulled back when she heard a sob, but Myrtle still kept eye contact, wanting the physical closeness of a friend; of someone who cared about her.

"Sorry, I shouldn't cry... it's just," another sob fled from Myrtle, "this is the first time I've felt loved in years." Myrtle looked to the floor, a smile on her face despite the tears dropping. She was going to try, from now on. If people wouldn't forgive her, she'd need to work to earn their trust back. That was what Ellen had taught her. Even if people had terrible preconceived ideas about her, she could change from who they thought she was.

Meanwhile...

James turned to speak to Gak and Aria as Midnight began to walk over to the three, each of them knew they needed to have a talk and explain what had happened to them, slowly putting the pieces together.

Midnight's appearance had caught James off guard, he knew that many secrets had been hidden from him... but Midnight still being in Zelpha?

~THE SECRETS OF ZELPHA~

"Midnight? I thought..." James said, holding her arm to ensure his senses that she was really standing ahead of him. His past teammate was really standing right in front of him.

James' story at Zelpha wasn't quite the one you'd expect. From 2023 the groups changed from teams of two to teams of three. However, James and Midnight had won The Games of 2023, he was expecting to go home and not have this change affect him. The day after they won James woke up in his dorm to see that Midnight wasn't there, with no explanation as to why. He had worried all day, but when he couldn't find her he assumed she had managed to escape home. Ms Gaunt confirmed with him that Midnight had been sent home, but no information had been shared on James' escape. James spent the morning getting books from Miss Yonda's classroom waiting to hear from Ms Gaunt how he would be able to leave Zelpha, and it was then that he was reunited with his sister.

"Look, we are going to explain..." Midnight started with and hugged him. "We were *both* supposed to go home..."

James looked at her realising his thoughts had been right all this time, it wasn't just Midnight going home.

"That's what I thought..." he mumbled. Midnight began to kick her feet looking at the ground, realising she had to just state what had happened to her, putting it plain and simple.

"Ms Gaunt put us in the jails." She gestured towards Aria while still looking up at her old teammate.

~THE SECRETS OF ZELPHA~

"WHAT!" James shouted at the top of his lungs, he was very angry at this entire situation. Aria's face filled with fury, and the second she spoke James knew that she was Aria, the one who had sent him all the help.

"Yeah, she did." she angrily stated. For a moment - James looked at Aria, mesmerised. This was the girl that had allowed him to survive his days in this world, and he just had to understand why.

"Aria, can you explain something to me?" James asked politely. If he had respect for anyone it was certainly her.

"What is it, James?" Aria asked, aware that the boy would be likely to have many questions for her.

"Why did you send us help? You don't even know who I am." He started to ramble, he had so many questions racing around his mind.

"A very long time ago Gak and I had our magic stripped from us, I managed to escape my cell one day - although I was still in the jails themselves - and get a hold of a crystal which had originated from Gak's magic. I then learnt that you were Midnight's teammate so I tried to help you." James smiled at her, pleased that she was willing to support him although he had no powers. "I used it to pretend to be you and warned Ellen to know about her situation and the dangers around her..." James looked down towards the floor no longer smiling at Aria, trying to think when this could have been. Until he realised.

~THE SECRETS OF ZELPHA~

"So when she said she saw me in the library that one night, was it because of you?" He asked, quite stern that is had really just been her this whole time but glad that she was able to help prepare his little sister for this mess of a school.

"Yeah..." she quietly mumbled. There was a moment of silence until Gak decided to join the conversation with his point of view.

"From what I gathered - you and Midnight were supposed to be thrown in the jail... but we don't know why you specifically weren't. Ms Gaunt never told anyone why." he looked around at the three hoping that one of them had the answer.

"What about Aria?" James' eyes moved between all three standing around him. "She was in jail, right?" As soon as James said that Gak looked down to the floor, James had never seen anyone look so upset before - particularly Gak.

Suddenly, Aria - who seemed a calm and sweet young lady - became very aggressive in her tone.

"Look... I am a sweet girl but when it comes to that witch I shall have no sympathy. She put me in that cell twenty-six years ago and separated me from my twin brother. He's my only family! He's the only one who loved me, and she separated us just because she had an argument with some Ferryman and didn't want to talk to him!" she ranted very quickly and angrily. Gak put his hand on her arm in an attempt to calm her down.

"Aria, we'll talk to her, but for now please try to stay calm."

~THE SECRETS OF ZELPHA~

Meanwhile...

Finishing her conversation with Myrtle, Ellen walked back over to the group which now contained the green team, Coverly, Gale, and Nyx.

"I think it might be time for you three to go home. I think we said our peace and kinda let out our emotions." Yadira stated quietly and rested her hand on Nyx's shoulder. Ellen began to scan the room for James and Dusk. However, she was held to a halt when Bridget began crying very loudly once again and dropped all of her weight into a hug to Ellen.

"I'm not done! I'll miss you so much rainbow hair!" She tried to exclaim while submerged in tears. In an attempt to calm Bridget, Ellen placed her hand on Bridget's arm and spoke to her.

"You know what, I'll miss you too Bridget, you and your silly nicknames." Ellen's attempt hadn't worked at all, in fact it caused Bridget to cry even louder, now wailing - gaining the entire castle grounds attention. Ellen's face was now as bright as the sun, and all of her friends held back their giggles. It was now that James had walked away from Gak, Aria and Midnight to reunite himself with his sister and his friends.

Although hidden, Nyx was feeling very emotional about the whole situation. This world and these people were all he knew from his entire life. He didn't know what to expect elsewhere in the world, let alone a different dimension. He

~THE SECRETS OF ZELPHA~

attempted to ignore Ellen and Bridget and talk to the others in a more serious tone.

"Yeah, I think it's time. I guess this is our final goodbye." he started. They all went around hugging one another and said their final goodbyes.

"Sorry for stealing your food mate," James mumbled to Gale with a hint of seriousness in his voice.

"It's alright, you owe me though," Gale said giggling.

"Yeah, I'm like sooo sorry," James responded, now sarcastically and playfully pushing Gale once again, in response he pushed James towards the castle exit.

Dusk ran towards the group, out of breath you could clearly see behind her was Evelyn, they had finally got the chance to speak to eachother once again. Myrtle had stopped controlling her. Duk was out of breath from running, she didn't want to miss them going home and not being able to say goodbye.

"You can't leave without a goodbye hug. Do some research into traveling through dimensions James, then we can see each other again," said Dusk, giving each of the blue team a very quick hug, knowing they most likely want to escape Ms Gaunt's wrath as soon as humanly possible. James nodded in response until Coverly asked,

"And publish the book, James. Did you find the village?" James explained that they had found the village and that he would get the book published as soon as he could. He then began

~THE SECRETS OF ZELPHA~

to jokingly whine about all the requests the girls had for him and not his teammates.

"Do I not get a job?" Ellen asked.

"Yeah and me!" Nyx added. Coverly looked at the two and put her hand on Nyx's shoulder.

"Look after yourselves, never forget us." she requested of the two. Slowly beginning to turn around, Nyx finished talking to Coverly.

"How could I forget you Cove?!" He said, reaching his hand out to her as he slowly walked closer and closer to the exit.

"Goodbye, Ellen," Myrtle muttered under her breath, looking at the young girl who was walking closer and closer to the door, closer and closer to never seeing Myrtle again.

Unaware that Ellen had heard her, she started to walk away until she was tackled into a hug. She recognised the feeling of who was behind her straight away, the feeling of true love had reached her once again.

"Stay safe okay, don't worry I'll sort everything for you with the others, I promise." As Ellen spoke a spark of magic hovered around Ellen's hand. Myrtle realised that Ellen would speak to her friends telepathically.

"I trust you, thank you for that little bit of love." Those were the last words Myrtle said while looking into Ellen's eyes. Myrtle gently cried with Bridget loudly sobbing behind her, Yadira had her arm around Bridget. Ellen, James and Nyx exited the castle as Myrtle inched closer and closer to her old friends.

~THE SECRETS OF ZELPHA~

Silence rang in the air as the three walked towards the area where the Ferryman was said to wait. James looked ahead with purpose, while Ellen and Nyx looked around the area they were walking.

As the group made their way towards the area Ms Gaunt had instructed them to go to, they saw a strange fellow. He was looking out into the sunset. The three stood still, looking at him. He wore a yellowish orange outfit, with a purple cape resting over his head dangling to the floor. The surroundings were the most beautiful landscape the group had ever seen. The forest illuminated the area and the sun was slowly inching further down. The Ferryman had a small blanket with some barrels located by the dock with his boat. His little area rested underneath a huge willow tree, with berries and lights hanging from it. The three students walked over and their footsteps caught the Ferryman's attention. He majestically turned to face the group.

"What did I do to owe the pleasure of seeing you three? Has The Game already passed and gone away?" his accent was one like no other, he was only just understandable to the three; sounding old and frail. The three looked at each other, realising they hadn't planned what to say, that was until Nyx stepped forward and began to speak.

"We have a request if you will." The Ferryman now took these people seriously and tried to straighten his posture a little when responding back.

~THE SECRETS OF ZELPHA~

"Oh? Pray tell this request?" he answered back to the student ahead of him. That was until James spoke, the Ferryman turned up to the boy who was towering over him.

"Our headteacher has requested us to go home," he stated confidently, not realising his words had actions, and not the ones he expected. The Ferryman stared back in confusion.

"Huh? And why shall I let you three go home? The rules state only one may pass onto my boat." he said with a little anger starting to show in his tone. Ellen didn't like the hint of anger hidden deep within his tone, especially when it was aimed at her brother; she plucked the courage to join the conversation.

"It's because we are the blue team and-" the Ferryman spoke over her with a laugh, that hint of anger now nowhere to be seen.

"Ah yes, the blue team. I agree to do what your headteacher has asked of me," he said with a big smile on his face as he clapped his hands together.

"Wait really?!" James shouted back. He would be able to go home and work hard, selling crops to buy flowers to put wherever his mother had been laid to rest. He could go home and see Chester, be with his little sister; be like a family once again. Realising he could gain from this, the Ferryman proposed a deal to the group.

"Of course, all I ask is that in order for me to do as you request - you must speak to the Wizard. Then will I be able to send you home?" The Ferryman continued to speak in a strange

~THE SECRETS OF ZELPHA~

manner - as though he had not properly learnt the language. Nyx tried to talk in a similar manner - hoping to keep him civil.

"Thank you sir Ferryman... wait do you know how we shall locate this Wizard fellow?" he asked curiously.

"Yes, his home is quite unique so you will know immediately. His home is quite a lovely hut if I must say so." Nyx was disappointed as the Ferryman hadn't fully answered his question; that was until he pointed in the direction of the path they took to The Games. They thanked the Ferryman, leaving with a polite wave, walking down the path they had been told to go. Partway through their journey they realised that they had to go over the river, away from The Games area. The three walked in silence, left to their own thoughts.

After what seemed like a never-ending treacherous journey, James laid eyes on the hut which was a simple path away from him.

"So, this must be the Wizard's hut. The Ferryman did say it was quite unique, I see he's not wrong," James stated as the other two looked up at what would be the next step in their journey.

Looking down the mud path with crystals, trees, rocks and farms surrounding it, Ellen saw a dark wooden hut with supports attached to it. The roof was pointed upwards in a gable-roofed style all over. Several windows dotted around the whole building showed Ellen the mess that was hidden within

~THE SECRETS OF ZELPHA~

the walls. On a balcony located above the entrance, they all spotted the Wizard walking back into his house.

The sudden disappearance of the man made all three slightly tense, looking at one another simply waiting for someone to speak.

"Do we just knock on the door?" Nyx asked in a hushed tone. Ellen - who was already several steps ahead of the others - quietly knocked on the door of the mysterious man's hut. The door had been opened half an inch and the same Wizard's face looked at Ellen through the small gap.

"Excuse me Sir Wizard, we have been asked to speak with you." Ellen asked quite confidently, standing out in the tense environment around her.

The Wizard quietly grumbled to himself on the other side of the door. He never got visitors and struggled to trust anyone that considered knocking on his door - this was the life of a misunderstood man.

"Yes, yes. At least you people are polite and not banging on my door," he said so quietly it was almost as though he was speaking to himself. He opened the door very slowly - peering at all three who were now standing on his open-planned porch. "What lot do you need of me?" he asked - clearly displeased that he had visitors.

"We were told by the Ferryman to talk to you about allowing the three of us to go home." Nyx finally spoke, entering the Wizard's hut. The Wizard's face lit up as soon as he heard

~THE SECRETS OF ZELPHA~

'Ferryman'. He knew this day would eventually come, but after all of these years, it felt as though it never would.

"Ah yes! Now, what you need is the crystals," he said in a much more contented tone. Now more comfortable the Wizard sat at his table at the other side of his small hut.

"Crystals?" James questioned, finally ready to talk to the Wizard.

"Yes, now please listen carefully. I ask you three to gather these shards from the village nearby." The Wizard stated, pointing in the direction of the village out of his window.

This was when Ellen realised, the village he spoke of was the one the group had previously discovered - the magical beings one. Trying to stay rational, Ellen simply asked the Wizard if she was correct, and indeed she was. The three looked at each other with disquietude quickly filling their eyes. They were aware of how the non-magicals would treat humans without magic.

After a moment of looking for reassurance in each other's eyes, they all nodded to the Wizard as they couldn't trust their dry-throated voices at this moment in time.

"Alrighty then." The Wizard quickly stood up, his chair scratching on the floor as he pushed it back under the desk and started walking to the door. "As soon as you've gathered them, please come back here," he requested.

The three left the Wizard's hut quietly, Ellen closing the door behind them firmly. Nyx - who had been in deep thought since entering the Wizard's hut - sighed and spoke, startling

~THE SECRETS OF ZELPHA~

Ellen and James who hadn't heard anything out of him for the past few minutes.

"I-I think it would be best for me to stay in Zelpha..." Nyx stated hesitantly, shocking both people he held the hands of.

"But why?!" James asked.

"Nyx?! We've got this far... Why now? We are almost home, we've just got to do this one last thing!" Ellen added with concern.

Nyx was proud of who he had become in Zelpha, whether Nyx was his name, red was his favourite colour, he made his mechanical wings or not he had created his entire personality in just four days and he liked it. If this is the world and dimension that had allowed him to become this young man then that is where he wanted to stay. He had been happy these past four days, Gak and Midnight meant the world to him, Mr Gallo was like a father to him, and this place started to feel like home. Just because these people had memories going back decades and Nyx was just a small part of their lives doesn't mean Nyx was prepared to lose the only people he knew. He didn't know enough about Ellen and James to decide that he wanted to live their Overworlder lifestyle. He just wanted to escape the school and run away as far as his legs could take him.

"That's the thing!! We have been told time after time 'magical beings will hurt us', 'everyone must have magic', and 'we will go home'. What about when they find out we don't have

~THE SECRETS OF ZELPHA~

magic?" Nyx shouted in Ellen's face, violently pushing her hand away. As Nyx continued to yell he got closer to Ellen's face. James got more and more angry as Nyx was shouting, eventually shoving him off Ellen. He stood in front of Nyx pointing his finger in his face.

"If you are going to go close to Ellen, do not and I repeat - do *not* yell in her face." James put his arm back by his side. "I know we are all stressed but it is completely unacceptable to yell in my sister's face, your own friend's face. You must be insane!!" Not wanting to repeat the actions of Nyx, James turned to Ellen, grabbing her hand. "You know what, come on Ellen. Let's leave him, if he wants to join he can but he must apologise for doing such vile things first." and with that, James dragged Ellen away from the situation.

Nyx looked at the two siblings as they got further and further away, slowly out of his eyesight. He sat on the grassy floor, leaning against a tree by the Wizard's hut as a few tears of guilt dropped from his eyes. He didn't want to leave just yet - Zelpha was the only life he knew.

"I swear, we can do this without him. If he wants to be all talk-" James shouted to himself, still dragging Ellen.

"James... JAMES! Let go of my wrist!" She spun him round before he let go so he could look her in the eye. He stood staring at his younger sister in shock at the volume of her voice.

~253~

~THE SECRETS OF ZELPHA~

"I get it you're angry but at least don't hold my wrist hostage..." she said in her normal tone rubbing the red mark on her wrist.

"I-I'm so sorry Ellen," James sighed. "I just didn't know what to do so I had to get you away from him." James apologised, in shock at how far he let his protectiveness get.

"All good, just please don't hold a grudge against Nyx," Ellen asked. They were at the last step and she knew he would not forgive Nyx unless Ellen requested.

"Oh, I will. Not a horrible one - as long as he apologises for the scene he made. I'll act civil until he earns my trust again." he stated very firmly, still vexed.

"James..." Ellen said quietly.

"Oh alright. You know that I just don't like when people talk to you that way, especially that he was talking to you specifically. I do not allow people to do such things." James was very overprotective of his sister, after all he had been through she was always there for him. Whether it was at home, searching day and night for him, or in a completely different dimension.

"I know. Right then, when do you think we will get close to the village?" Ellen swiftly moved on, trying not to complain about the tiredness in her legs from being dragged at James' long-legged steps.

"I have a feeling it's only going to be a few more minutes before-" Ellen cut James off,

~THE SECRETS OF ZELPHA~

"I see it!" She shouted recalling the buildings and pathways from when she last looked here with Nyx. The last time she looked at this village, her eyes had been flooded with tears from being on the topic of her mother. The one by her side was Nyx, she knew she couldn't leave without him.

"Well, I spoke too soon I guess," James added, walking into the village. As they walked deeper into the village they realised it had been overgrown with plant life and was quite deteriorated, to say the least. The scene lying in front of their eyes was the aftermath of war. The two looked down, the way war warps your mind. Warps your mind so badly you don't even think that you may be killing the life of someone who was a really good being, someone who improved the world around them. They knew they couldn't sit here weeping now, they had to get out of here as soon as possible.

"I think this place may be deserted, look at the fountain. It's completely dry. Wait... is that a book on a lectern over there?" It was at this moment that Ellen realised the Wizard had not instructed the group on what to do once reaching the village, so they must go exploring for it. James questioned her and ran over to the lectern she had been pointing at. He grabbed the closed book and brushed off the thick layer of dust lying on top. Ellen quickly ran over to her brother, with much interest as to what was contained in the book James held.

~THE SECRETS OF ZELPHA~

"Let's see what's written" James said standing near his sister so they could both read the contents. Opening the front cover, the title read...

Hide and Seek - The Rules
Written by G, A, M and the Magical Beings.

"Hide and Seek?! Is this seriously just a rule book?! Huh?! There's more... 'We have hidden many shards within this village, the more you find - the more points you have.'" James read aloud.

"So like a game?" Ellen questioned herself, continuing to flick through the book. This book was certainly too thick to be for hide and seek alone.

"A magical game." James sighed, they wouldn't be able to take part, or even ask people for assistance. Their lack of magic had always been considered an issue, but Ellen and James always found a way. This time they did not need to.

"No look, it says here. 'A simple game of hide and seek' I wonder why they haven't excluded non-magicals?" Ellen looked up at James questioning him, then looked down at the book and read to him.

"Oh look, here 'we are unaware of what the future will hold, but at this current moment, non-magical beings and magical beings are united as one, with a strong friendship. This

~THE SECRETS OF ZELPHA~

is why we have kept this as a game where magic is not required. Allowing our non-magical pals to join us too. Enjoy the fun.'"

"Well, let's get to finding these crystals, and quick," Ellen said looking up at the sky realising the sun was about to set. The two set off on a journey, the crystals made a small humming sound, nothing too obnoxious but loud enough to be irritating to say the least so the siblings started running to find them. These crystals were everywhere, in trees, in abandoned homes, under floorbooards, you name it the biggest issue was how hidden they were in these areas. Although non-magicals were able to join in, it certainly wasnt easy without magic. After a short while Ellen checked in on how many James had found.

"Come on James! It's getting dark, how many do you have?" Ellen stopped again, panting heavily. Her voice was faint but assertive. She saw James, who was only a small distance away from her, glare at her before stopping to catch his breath as well. Ellen knew that James was pondering on what to reply to her question before getting back to running around. James' hair was a mess from running around and full of sweat.

"Four, but monsters come out at night. How many do you have?" James responded hoping he couloud stop all the running. Unlike his sister he didn't always have energy to be running around.

Ellen grumbled a bit, stumbling again on her own feet. She got back up and ran towards another shed-like structure before replying to her brother. Even though she was taking breaks from running, it felt like she was not catching her breath at all.

" I've got five! Come on, we need a total of ten!" Finally able to catch her breath, Ellen stopped running after giving her reply.

"Found it!" James exclaimed, his voice sounding hoarse from exhasution.

After all the running around, Ellen just wanted to sleep for hours. She sighed before walking closer to James as he put the last crystal in his pocket. James let out a huge sigh as his breathing slowed. One of his sentences caught her attention before she was distracted, so she brought it up.

"Thank God for that! What did you say about monsters?" She questioned him. Realising what she meant, James replied back.

"It's not specified whether they are magic or non-magical, but either way they come out at night; without the best of intentions for anyone. Magic aside, we need to get to safety." James stated as he walked closer to Ellen.

Ellen huffed as she pondered on where to take shelter, going through her memories of the day's events - she did remember that there was somewhere that they could at least sit down. James just glanced at her, wondering what she was thinking about - as the face she was making was one that he knew well.

~THE SECRETS OF ZELPHA~

"I found a cave on the way here, it seemed like some abandoned home," Ellen told her brother.

James thought for a bit, trying to think of the pros and cons before realising that they really did need shelter now and he was certainly not comfortable sleeping in a magical beings house knowing he could have been the one to slaughter it. He knew that Ellen needed her sleep and so did he. He sighed before nodding at her, deciding that it was for the best.

"Let's go there, for the night then." He responded. Ellen smiled before starting to walk towards the location. James noted down that he knew some of the surroundings from all the running he did. Even though Ellen knew the way, they found themselves retracing their steps about twice before reaching their destination. They finally found the place Ellen mentioned - which turned out to be a small cave.

Once they had reached it they discovered that Ellen was right, it had actually been an abandoned home. They could tell because there was a small barrel in the corner of the cave. They searched through its contents. Inside lay two blankets, a lantern and a few pieces of old paper. The discolouration of the paper made it clear to Ellen that this had been here a very long time. They reached out and grabbed the blankets, James' was a dark blue and Ellen's was tattered and grey.

"I'm worried about Nyx," Ellen commented, beginning to lie down on her blanket, in an attempt to get comfortable.

~THE SECRETS OF ZELPHA~

"He will be fine Ellen, I'm not letting you go back out there just get some rest."

Listening to James, Ellen snuggled up close to her blanket. As she hugged her blanket, she finally felt a feeling of safety, and that's when she realised it had been quite some time since she had felt that comforting feeling.

"This reminds me of my blanket at home..." Ellen mumbled before sheprepared to get some sleep, she needed to end the night on a lighter tone so she wasn't up all night thinking of Nyx.

"You always loved that blanket" James responded staring straight up at the cave roof, without a single feeling of sleepiness, eventhough he was exhausted from all of the running his mind was still wheezing around with thoughts and things to say.

Ellen had a look of happiness, but in her eyes, you could see small tears there.

"You remember?" Ellen said, looking James in the eye. They looked at each other with the memories of life before they came here, the memories that they hadn't had the chance to discuss even once these past four days.

"Of course I do, it meant the world to you, I think you loved it more than me." He said this while laughing. Ellen got a little embarrassed by what he had just said, she turned to him and spurted out.

~THE SECRETS OF ZELPHA~

"Oh shush, I was actually going to throw that away before coming here," Ellen said with a hint of embarrassment in her voice.

"Why!?" James questioned her, he was sure that the blanket was important to her, even if it was old and scratchy.

"I thought you wouldn't have remembered it, it made me too upset." Ellen sadly replied.

James looked at Ellen with a comforting look making sure Ellen understood that he cared about her and wanted to make sure that she was happy, James said,

"Of course, I did, just know we will be going back home to that blanket soon. Now, try and get some rest." He said comfortingly. After hearing how much James cared about Ellen at that moment she felt she could finally relax and she was happy, Ellen looked and James and said,

"Fine."

They had fallen asleep on a cold and clear night. The atmosphere was peaceful and the sound of the wildlife outside their cave was therapeutic.

The following morning, Ellen awoke and squinted with the sun in her eyes.

"James, wake up. We must go to the Wizard." She mumbled, with her eyes still closed. James had been waiting for Ellen to open her eyes and get up to see who was standing next to him. He said,

"I'm already awake, silly, and I found someone."

~THE SECRETS OF ZELPHA~

Ellen rubbed her eyes to see James sat on the cold floor with none other then Nyx sat beside him. They had the blanket James had used to sleep wrapped around them. It was so cold in this cave that they needed to find some warth, thankfully they had eachothers body heat to keep captured.

"Oh my gosh you're okay" Ellen shouted, now sitting upright. Nyx looked happy to see Ellen and said to her happily,

"James and I spoke, I'm so sorry. I don't know what came over me! Thanks for caring about me though, he said you mentioned me a few times." Nyx smiled, he may have loved Mr Gallo like a father and Gak and Midnight like best friends but he loved these two like they were his own blood. They all looked at each other with happiness flooding over them and Ellen went to say something to Nyx,

"Of course! Anyway, it's fine, as long as everyone is okay that's all that matters."

Ellen sat in silence for a moment, taking the time to fully wake up. Eventually, all three got off the ground and began to walk to the Wizard's hut once again.

"Nyx, We will not leave here without you - you know that right?" James said now feeling bad about arguing back to Nyx. He regretted his decision, but also still didn't know what was the right thing to do then, until Nyx began to speak.

"I just thought after I yelled at you - you guys would be better off without me. This isn't my homeworld after all." Nyx looked down, disappointed in himself and regretting his actions majorly.

"Never, you're our friend - even kind of like a sibling... considering how we act with each other," Ellen said, putting her arm around Nyx's shoulder for comfort.

"Wait... did we just have our first sibling fight... we did, didn't we." James joked in an attempt to lift the mood. All three began to laugh at the revelation.

"Yeah, I think going home all as a group is better than staying in some castle." An awkward silence lingered in the air until Nyx started the conversation once again,

"So, uhm, how did gathering the shards go?"

"Surprisingly, it was a simple game of hide and seek with the crystals. There was nobody at the village." Ellen replied.

"The funny thing about it is that a book we found said that when the game was made, non-magicals and magicals were united... I still wonder what happened between them." James shrugged at his own comment, knowing he wasn't ever going to find out. It was left to his imagination.

The three made a bit of small talk on their way to the Wizard's hut, in an attempt to fill the awkward silence. After what felt like a year of walking they had reached their destination. James knocked on the door, announcing that they were back.

~THE SECRETS OF ZELPHA~

"Ah, glad to see you lot again. Do you have the shards I have requested?" He asked while letting the three of them with a large smile plastered on his face.

"Yes sir!" Nyx said, pointing at the bundle of crystals in James' hands.

"Lovely, lovely. Thank you." As the Wizard spoke, James handed the bundle to him. The Wizard walked over to the desk he sat at when the three last spoke to him and dumped them down.

"Now, I do hope that with this crystal you people are able to go home." The Wizard said kindly, he knew these students were very well-behaved and deserved to escape this world.

"I do hope so, I just want to rest in a place where I don't have to play some stupid games," Nyx responded kicking his feet. He was fed up with this world, the only world he knew.

"Don't worry child, knowing the Ferryman - he will keep his promise. Now you better be off, off to your homeworlds." He shook each student's hand and with that, the Wizard bowed before them and disappeared into a puff of smoke. The three looked in awe before turning around to leave the hut, shutting the heavy dark wooden door behind them. The three walked together, making small chit-chat until they caught the Ferryman's eye. James - who was holding the crystal ran towards the Ferryman with a smile.

"Ferryman! Ferryman!" James shouted out of breath still running towards him. He came to a halt standing right in front

~THE SECRETS OF ZELPHA~

of the man ahead. "We have the crystal!" He finished saying with the glowing object sitting in his hand, seeping light through his fingers. The Ferryman's mysterious smile grew bigger and bigger on his face as he went to grab it out of James' hand.

"Oh really? How lovely! Hand it over shall you?" As he went to grab it Mr Gallo and Gak ran into the scene.

Gak dived into the Ferryman, knocking him to the ground. He kept him pinned down and looked at James whose face was now filled with concern. Gak brushed his hair out of his face with his fingers, keeping one hand on the Ferryman.

"Stop! James, don't do it!" Mr Gallo screamed at James. The young boy too stunned to speak stood pale white.

"Why? What's up?" Nyx questioned, they had spent so long getting to their final destination what was in their way this time? Mr Gallo turned to Nyx, still covering James' hand. Whilst all this was going on James continued to take several small steps backwards, trying to escape the scene.

"I've just spoken to Gaunt and-" The Ferryman who now heard the name 'Gaunt' tried to wriggle free to look at Mr Gallo. He was unable to stand up but shouted.

"Gaunt?!" He looked at Mr Gallo intensely and realised he recognized the man. He knew Mr Gallo from the days when he was a student, best friend and teammate of the kindest students at Zelpha, Jane Gaunt. Until she changed, one single argument between Jane Gaunt, The Ferryman and David Gallo changed the ways of Zelpha, forever.

~THE SECRETS OF ZELPHA~

"-she's told me he's wanted this for years! He's a danger with it." The three students now faced the situation that formed in front of their eyes.

"Me? No, no, no- I am no danger," The Ferryman argued back, still on the floor.

"You've had a cold war with the poor woman for so long!" Gak stood up to show his dominance over the Ferryman, therefore allowing the man to stand up. Gak now turned and looked at James, pleadingly. "Just don't do it. Please." James stood concerned, not knowing what to do.

"What do we even do?" Nyx questioned.

"We want to go home, Mr Gallo!" James shouted.

"Let us! All three of us!" Nyx wailed loudly.

"No!" Mr Gallo argued back.

"Yes! We want to go back home." James argued. All of the shouting was layered overtop of each other, nobody could understand anyone. Ellen couldn't think, so instead she screamed her thoughts aloud.

"Everyone shut up!" she shouted over each of them, silencing everyone. "Shut up! Look, we want to go home. You don't want him to have the crystal. Here's the deal, the Ferryman takes us home and then we leave the crystal on his boat, and he will agree not to touch it. Then we are home and it's a conflict left between you on what happens." The group looked at each other, silent. Until the Ferryman felt like he must argue against this, this was not the deal he had agreed to,

~THE SECRETS OF ZELPHA~

"Child please, you are giving me that crystal - that was the deal." Nyx pushed his way to stand in the Ferryman's face and shouted,

"We saved your goddamn life!" With a sigh, the Ferryman agreed to the deal and nodded his head.

"Well, fine then. I shall deal with you and that lovely Gaunt at another point in time." The three students started to walk towards the Ferryman.

"There's nothing we can do sir, they want to leave. Let them." Mr Gallo sighed, as a sign of acceptance before Gak continued talking. "Ellen, before you go. You seemed so... interested in this. So, as a memory, The Secrets of Zelpha." with that Gak passed his first copy of his book to Ellen. His book named The Secrets of Zelpha. Ellen reached her hands out to hold it and look at the front cover, she smiled gratefully and Gak gave her a nod. His nod explained that it was hers to keep. The Ferryman looked at the three that walked down the dock towards him. He waved his hand in the direction of his small boat and smiled softly.

"One by one please, I shall see you soon Gaunt." One by one; Ellen, James and Nyx stepped onto the boat, taking their seats. They looked back at Gak and Mr Gallo who waved at all four of them, sad to see them go. Suddenly, their surroundings went bright white blinding all three. Then everything went black and their voices became echoey.

~THE SECRETS OF ZELPHA~

"W-what happened?" Nyx questioned them. His voice stuttered with a hint of worry and fear.

"Where are we?" James asked the group, James was confused about what was going on. Ellen began to speak,

"Home."

~THE SECRETS OF ZELPHA~

Open this when you are ready Ellen - Mother

Hello Rainbow, my time with you has been incredible, and full of wonderful memories that we collected during our time together, but our chapter has come to an end. I can't bear to imagine you alone, just you and Chester... Please look after him for me. He gave the whole family a bunch of laughs and close times and I hope he continues to bring big smiles to your face.

    I need to tell you this now, and although we have been told your brother has passed away, part of me wishes that he isn't truly gone, he's still out there somewhere, fighting for his own turf. It may just be me in denial of his death, but if you agree with me, we can both expect that he's still walking... please, find him, do anything to try and find his lost soul, even if it's lost in the darkness. Look after him for me, he has struggled with many things throughout his life and I'm sure all he wants is his little sister to comfort him after the cold journey he's been trenching through. Since the day he could speak, he always spoke about having a sister, someone to love, someone to care for... he loved you before you were even a part of our lives. Please look after him when you find him, also make sure that you look after yourself too.

~THE SECRETS OF ZELPHA~

You have been through so much, especially since the night of the storm.

As I age, my memory slowly fades away, but within those memories, our time together stays intact. I remember sitting with a book and Chester on the sofa, while James was out with you picking berries. I recall hearing them all fall to the ground as James rushed you inside, the storm had started. I had to find a distraction for you two, yes I know you were teenagers but you were still young and scared, this storm was insane, right over our roof. I started by having us all make hot chocolates. I had found the money to buy your favourite marshmallows the night before and I knew this was the best time to put them to use. The two of you sat on the scratchy, old rug with your drinks while I read you a book. I remember closing the torn old curtains and putting on our small lamp to hide the lightning. Chester was lying on his back with all four paws in the air as perusal, and I read book after book to the both of you. The storm began to settle down, still ongoing but more distant, so you two went to bed. As you headed up the stairs James came to me, hugged me and thanked me. Who knows maybe he's out there somewhere reading books. About fifteen minutes later Chester and I went to bed.

~THE SECRETS OF ZELPHA~

I remember hearing the crash in James' room, it woke me instantly, and I ran straight to him. The tree had collapsed into the house, so I called for you. You were sitting awake crying, with Chester on your bed. We lifted the branch from his bed, but he wasn't there. I ran outside screaming his name and you followed on. I remember telling you to go back inside, it was too dangerous to be out in the nightmare of a storm. That's when I realised... Chester was gone, our family, our lives, our home... it was all falling apart. I saw you and held you tight, calling his name. He was nowhere, and that became the new normal, searching.

I am so sorry that I am no longer there to look after you, I'm sure that you will do your best on your own even though you need the support of your mother. I am glad we found Chester now, some company, some family, is better than none.

I will forever hold gratitude that you both were mine and I will take that love and gratitude with me when I go.

I love you,
Mum xxxx

Printed in Great Britain
by Amazon